"Can you tell me about the murders he was convicted of?"

"One woman was a bank teller. He attacked her outside her apartment building one night. A month later, he attacked a couple—a man and a woman—at a park." Jake's jaw tightened, lips compressed and pale.

"Is there something else?" she asked. "Something you aren't telling me?" She leaned toward him across the table. "I want to know. I'm not going to freak out, I promise."

He exhaled a long breath, then reached over and switched off the recording. "This doesn't go any further than this room," he said.

She nodded. "I promise I won't tell a soul."

"Cutler was convicted of killing the three people I mentioned, but he's a suspect for five other murders, at least. He was being transported to Junction to be tried in one of those cases. All women." He swallowed, Adam's apple bobbing, then met and held her gaze. "The Bernalillo County Sheriff's department sent over a file, with photographs of his suspected victims. All women in their twenties and thirties, athletic builds, with blue eyes and reddish hair."

She drew a sharp breath. The women he had described... "They all look like me," she whispered.

EAGLE MOUNTAIN CLIFFHANGER

CINDI MYERS

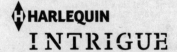

HARLEQUIN
INTRIGUE

For the Ouray Mountain Rescue Team.

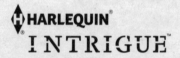

Recycling programs
for this product may
not exist in your area.

ISBN-13: 978-1-335-58302-4

Eagle Mountain Cliffhanger

Copyright © 2022 by Cynthia Myers

For questions and comments about the quality of this book, please contact us at CustomerService@Harlequin.com.

Harlequin Enterprises ULC
22 Adelaide St. West, 41st Floor
Toronto, Ontario M5H 4E3, Canada
www.Harlequin.com

Printed in U.S.A.

Cindi Myers is the author of more than fifty novels. When she's not plotting new romance story lines, she enjoys skiing, gardening, cooking, crafting and daydreaming. A lover of small-town life, she lives with her husband and two spoiled dogs in the Colorado mountains.

Books by Cindi Myers

Harlequin Intrigue

Eagle Mountain Search and Rescue

Eagle Mountain Cliffhanger

Eagle Mountain: Search for Suspects

Disappearance at Dakota Ridge
Conspiracy in the Rockies
Missing at Full Moon Mine
Grizzly Creek Standoff

The Ranger Brigade: Rocky Mountain Manhunt

Investigation in Black Canyon
Mountain of Evidence
Mountain Investigation
Presumed Deadly

Eagle Mountain Murder Mystery:
Winter Storm Wedding

Ice Cold Killer
Snowbound Suspicion
Cold Conspiracy
Snowblind Justice

Visit the Author Profile page at Harlequin.com.

CAST OF CHARACTERS

Hannah Richards—A paramedic and SAR volunteer, Hannah lives at the inn her family runs and longs for a more settled existence with a home and family of her own. That dream is threatened when she is targeted by a serial killer.

Jake Gwynn—The newest deputy with the Rayford County Sheriff's Department plans to use the job as a stepping-stone to bigger and better things—until the hunt for a killer sidetracks him and makes him look at his life differently.

Danny Irwin—Hannah's former lover and fellow SAR volunteer who still has feelings for her.

Charles Cutler—The convicted serial killer has nothing to lose when he escapes in the wilderness outside of Eagle Mountain, though he is soon stalking his next victim.

Chapter One

Hannah Richards accelerated up the mountain road in her battered Subaru, torn between wanting to hurry and the need for caution on the narrow, winding lanes. A callout for Search and Rescue always fired her adrenaline, and a swift response could mean the difference between life and death. But experience working in these mountains made her hyperaware of the hazards that lurked in the picturesque setting. Snow softened the sharp edges of the landscape around her, like a puffy white comforter draped over the ridges of the surrounding mountains. The road was a thin black ribbon wound around the peaks, with no guardrails separating the narrow shoulder and the deep ravine to her right.

She took her foot off the gas as she neared a pullout that offered a view of the frozen waterfall and the canyon below, a popular photo spot. The motorist who had called to report the accident said the van had gone off the road just past this pull off. Yes, there was a set of tire tracks gouged deep in the snow, veering off the road and into the ravine below.

Hannah stopped the Subaru and checked her rearview mirror. No one coming. Carefully, she backed to the pullout and parked, then hurried to get out and collect her gear bag from the back. As a paramedic, she always traveled prepared for an emergency. She had been out shopping when the call from the 911 dispatcher came in, which had allowed her to be first on the scene. But if the van was very far down in the ravine, she'd have to wait for a climbing crew to determine the safest route down to her patients. Every member of Eagle Mountain Search and Rescue was trained in emergency first aid, but for serious cases—and driving off the side of a mountain definitely qualified as a serious case—it was up to the two paramedics, one nurse and one doctor on the SAR roster to deliver the kind of high-level care any survivor of this accident was likely to require.

She slung a pack with most of the supplies she might need over one shoulder and walked back to the spot where the tire tracks disappeared over the edge. As she walked, she checked her watch. The call from the motorist who had seen what he described as a "boxy white van" go over the side had come in approximately twenty minutes before. The outside temperature up here was twenty-one degrees. It would probably be colder in the ravine. Every minute counted if someone had managed to survive the plummet over the edge.

She walked alongside the tire tracks, post-holing through deep snow. A recent training exercise, conducted by the Rayford County Sheriff's Department, had stressed the importance of preserving evidence at the scene, in order to aid law enforcement in determining the cause of the accident. About a foot from where the ground fell away, Hannah stopped and peered over the edge.

The white van lay on its side about a hundred yards down the steep slope, resting against a large boulder. It looked as if a giant had hit it with a hammer—the top and sides dented in, steam pouring from beneath the crumpled hood. Hannah cupped her hands to either side of her mouth and shouted. "Hello! Can you hear me? I'm with Search and Rescue! Help is on the way!"

A scuffling noise to her left startled her, and she jumped back, heart pounding, and was amazed to see a man clambering up the slope toward her. Blood streamed down his face and drenched his clothing, mingling with the mud smeared on his hands and his pants from the knees down. At the sight of her, the man drew back and let out a groan.

He was probably in shock, or disoriented from what appeared to be a head wound. "It's okay." Hannah held out both hands. "I'm a paramedic. I'm here to help you. Can you tell me your name?"

The man stared at her, and she shrank from the menace in that look. People reacted strangely when they were in shock, she reminded herself. "My name's Hannah," she said. "You look like you're injured. I'd like to help."

A car door slammed and Hannah whirled to see a sheriff's deputy striding toward her. "What's the situation?" he called as he hurried toward her.

"The van is down there." She pointed down the slope. "And we've got at least one survivor. Sir, how many people—" But when she turned back toward the bleeding man, he had vanished.

"Sir!" She rushed toward where the man had been. "Sir!"

The sheriff's deputy moved in beside her. "A man was right here," she said. "He was climbing up the slope, and he was bleeding."

"Do you think he fell back down? It's pretty steep."

"Maybe." She could see the path the injured man had made through the snow coming up the slope, footprints and flecks of red on the snow marking his route. Had he descended the same way?

A siren announced the approach of a rescue vehicle. Relief surged through her when she recognized SAR Captain Tony Meissner and the vehicle they had termed the Beast, a specially modified Jeep that had seen better days, but held most of the team's gear—everything from oxygen tanks to a litter outfitted with oversize wheels for moving patients across rough ground, to equipment for extracting people from cars or hauling them out of mine tunnels, canyons or rivers.

Tony, a tall, bearded man in his late thirties who worked as a surveyor in his life outside SAR, was in his second year as leader of the search and rescue team. Calm and organized, he was good at quickly assessing a situation, and knew how to utilize each volunteer's strengths and compensate for their weaknesses.

With Tony was nurse Danny Irwin. Tall and lanky, with a mop of sandy hair, Danny had the weathered complexion of someone who spent all his spare time out of doors. Another medical person could come in handy if they had more than one victim with major trauma, though Hannah still felt a little awkward around him since their recent breakup after a brief affair. The split had been amicable, both of them agreeing they were better friends than lovers. But she was still learning to differentiate between what could sound like flirting and Danny's general charm.

"I'm Deputy Jake Gwynn." The sheriff's deputy stepped forward to introduce himself to Tony and Danny. He looked to be about Hannah's age—mid-twenties, with thick dark hair, dark brown eyes and high cheekbones. He had a handsome face that would make most people look twice.

"The new guy." Tony threw open the doors of the Beast and began hauling out ropes and other climbing equipment. "I remember you from the training a couple weeks ago." He looked past Gwynn to Hannah. "How far down is the vehicle?" he called.

"About a hundred yards," she said. "The slope is sixty to seventy degrees. The van is wedged against a big boulder, pretty smashed up. But there was at least one survivor. He was climbing up toward me, then he was gone."

"Could have lost consciousness and fallen." Danny came around to join Tony in pulling gear from the Beast. "We may have to climb down past the vehicle to find him."

"What can I do to help?" Gwynn asked.

"Traffic control," Tony said. "This road is too

narrow and dangerous to have people slowing down or even stopping to rubber-neck. We need you to move them along."

Two more vehicles pulled into the parking area behind Hannah's Subaru: volunteers Sheri Stevens and Ryan Welch piled out of Ryan's red Jeep, with Ted Carruthers tight behind them in a big black truck. Another sheriff's department vehicle soon joined them.

Danny and Ryan, whose curly auburn hair had earned him the nickname Red, began laying out the climbing gear. "I'll go down first," Sheri said. No one argued; the tall blonde was one of the team's best climbers.

"I'll go down alongside and run a line we can use as a handhold to bring up the Stokes basket," Tony said. "Ted, you monitor things up top. Hannah, you and Ryan come down after Sheri and I have had a chance to assess things."

"We need to find the man I saw," Hannah reminded him. "He had a head wound and probably other injuries. He might be disoriented."

"I'll go down and start a search for him," Danny said. He looked at Hannah. "Show me where you saw him coming up the slope."

While she walked over to show Danny, Deputy Gwynn and a fellow deputy put out cones to close off one lane of traffic. This forced any passing vehicles to move by at a crawl, but gave the team more room to work.

Gwynn rejoined them shortly after Danny and Sheri had started their climbs down. "If somebody will make note of the plate number of the vehicle, we can start searching for the name of the owner, who may be the driver," he said.

"I'll get it," Ted said, clipping into his harness. The oldest volunteer at sixty, Ted was a fit, wiry man with thick gray hair and a neat goatee.

Gwynn stood beside Hannah and watched the team members descend. Sheri moved rapidly, propelling herself with agility and speed, as if she was skipping down a well-worn trail instead of an icy sixty-degree slope. "I'm Jake," Gwynn said.

She nodded, her gaze still fixed on Sheri. "I'm Hannah."

"Have you been with Search and Rescue long?"

"Four years." She glanced at him. He looked fit. She'd heard through the grapevine that he was single—that kind of news traveled fast in a small town, where the dating pool was limited. Not that Hannah was actively looking, but she was single and didn't necessarily want to stay that way forever. Still, now was not the time to be flirting with the new guy.

If, indeed, he was flirting. Maybe, as a cop,

he was used to asking questions. "It's a volunteer position, right?" he asked. "What do you do the rest of the time?"

"I'm a paramedic, for the county." That was her paid position, but there was considerable overlap with SAR. If a SAR call went out when she was on duty as a paramedic, she was free to respond—on the clock, as it were—as long as she wasn't already involved with transporting or otherwise tending to a patient.

The hand-held radios they used to communicate over short distances—fancy walkie-talkies, really—crackled, and she keyed the mic of hers. "What have you got?" She'd bet it was Sheri, first on the scene. She had been the fastest on the descent.

"The driver is DOA," Sheri said. "Still strapped into the seat. There's a passenger, and I'm pretty sure he's dead, too. There's a lot of blood, like maybe he got sliced by windshield glass or a piece of metal. We're going to have to move the driver out of the way to get to him. Somebody send down the Jaws."

The hydraulic extractor and cutter, commonly known as the Jaws of Life, could spread open crushed metal, giving a team member more room to work on an injured person, or to extract a body or other items from the wreckage.

"I'll bring it," Hannah said, and went to collect the tool from the van.

The Jaws in its carrying case weighed about fifty-five pounds. Instead of trying to carry it and her medical pack, Hannah fastened a line to the handle of the carrying case, and tied it securely. She handed the free end of the line to Jake. "Feed this down to me," she instructed. Not waiting for his answer, she started climbing down.

Unlike Sheri, Hannah didn't particularly enjoy climbing. She did it because it was one of the requirements of the job, and she'd had plenty of training and opportunities for practice. She took her time, carefully placing her hands and feet, the cold of the snow seeping through her gloves and boots, though her waterproof pants and gloves did a good job of keeping out the wet. Every couple of steps down, she paused and tugged on the Jaws to drag it down alongside her. She didn't look down, counting on Sheri to alert her when she was almost to the wreck. As long as she kept her gaze focused directly in front of her, or up the way she had come, she didn't have to think about what could happen if she slipped on the steep, icy rock. Yes, she was in a safety harness tied off to a piton hammered in the rock above, which, she knew from her training, would catch and hold her if she fell. But the sensation of swinging free into space, while it exhilarated some climbers, like Sheri, filled Hannah with a terror she did not care to repeat anytime soon.

"Almost down." Sheri's voice, firm and confident, sounded close, and a few moments later Hannah felt her teammate's hands on her hips, steadying her to a stop. When she was sure Hannah was secure, Sheri moved over to unfasten the Jaws. Tony moved to help her and together the two of them worked the contraption into the crushed driver's side door.

Hannah inched her way around the vehicle, trying to see past the damage to the figure slumped in the passenger seat. A big Black man, so not the man she had seen up top. He looked like someone had dumped a bucket of red-brown paint down his front—the metallic stench of blood made her throat convulse. She was sure he was dead, but she called out to him anyway. "Hey, mister!" she shouted. "Can you hear me? I've come to help you." No response, but then she hadn't expected any.

Danny moved in beside her. "I found some tracks in the snow, but no sign of your wounded man," he said. "We'll have to search for him after we've got a better handle on things here." He moved away to begin stabilizing the vehicle, placing blocks and even anchors to, she hoped, keep it in place until they had removed everyone inside. He tossed her a chock and she wedged it firmly under the tire, then did the same for the other two tires she could reach, while he fastened one end of a heavy chain to the front axle and the other to a tree upslope.

It took another agonizing half hour to expand and cut away the metal around the door until it was wide enough for Tony to lean in and examine the driver. He backed out, shaking his head. "He's already cold," he said. "We'd better get him out now." Once rigor set in, it would be that much more difficult to move the body.

As soon as they had dragged the driver—white, overweight, with thinning blond hair and a lot of head trauma—onto the ground, Hannah scrambled into the van, ignoring the blood and gore, the broken glass and bits of metal. Up close, the man in the passenger seat looked even worse. He was young, maybe late twenties, and he was wearing a uniform. She wiped blood from the gold star on his chest. Law enforcement, though she couldn't make out what branch. She forced herself to reach in past the blood to feel for the pulse at his neck. She had heard all kinds of stories about people surviving horrific injuries, so you always had to check.

What she found this time made her draw back

in horror, with a yelp of protest. "What is it?" Sheri asked. "Are you hurt?"

Hannah scrambled backward out of the van, then stumbled over to the side and was promptly sick. Sheri patted her back. "It's okay," she murmured. "All of us have seen something at one time or another that made us lose it. Just give yourself a minute to pull yourself together."

With shaking hands, Hannah accepted the bottle of water Sheri passed her. She rinsed her mouth, then pressed cold hands to her cheek. "It was just shock," she said.

"You okay?" Tony joined them.

Hannah nodded. "The passenger is some kind of law enforcement officer," she said. "And I don't think he died in the crash."

Tony's eyes narrowed. "What do you mean?"

Hannah closed her eyes, verifying that her memory of what she had seen in there was correct. She forced the words out past the tightness in her throat. "I'm pretty sure his throat was cut," she said. "He was murdered."

Chapter Two

"We need a law enforcement presence on scene."

Jake was coiling up the rope he had used to help convey the Jaws of Life to the accident site when an older man, one of the SAR volunteers, approached. "Captain says we have a situation down below," the man said.

"What's happened?" Jake shoved the coil of rope into the back of the SAR Jeep and turned to face the older man.

The man—gray haired and craggy, with skin like leather, shook his head. "Tony thinks we might have a crime scene on our hands. He'd like you down there ASAP."

"Of course." He looked toward the drop-off. "I'll need help getting down there."

"Done much climbing before?"

Jake made a face. "Does the climbing wall at the gym count?"

The man shrugged. "It's something. I got a

harness for you over here." He gestured toward a black truck. "My name's Ted," he said as Jake followed him to the truck.

"I'm Deputy Jake Gwynn."

"Okay, Deputy Gwynn. We got you the harness. A helmet. Gloves." Ted shoved each of these items at Jake as he spoke. "Hold on tight, watch your step, don't look down. If you slip, the harness will catch you. Ryan is going to climb down alongside you and coach you through everything. You shouldn't have any problem."

Not if you'd done it before, Jake thought, as he buckled the helmet under his chin, then stepped into the harness and pulled it up around his hips. He was from Eastern Colorado—the flat part, with not a mountain in sight.

But he said nothing of this to his guide. "Over here." Ted led him to the edge of the drop-off and handed him a rope. "I'll be belaying up top here, and Ryan will be alongside, so you'll be fine."

Ryan wore a bright red helmet plastered with stickers for various outdoor equipment manufacturers. He clipped into a rope that ran parallel to Jake's. "Take it slow and listen to my instructions," he said. "If you get stuck, stop and wait for my help."

Though Jake's heart hammered with trepidation at the climb, he was also excited about what he might find at the wreck. He didn't want bad things to happen to people, but he liked the challenge of solving crimes and stopping bad guys.

Focusing thoughts on what he might find at the wreck helped him make it down the slope. That, and Ryan's firm coaching. The soles of his winter boots kept slipping in the mixture of mud and snow on the slope, but he held tight to the rope and managed to keep from falling. When he reached the place where the van had come to rest, the pretty redhead he'd met earlier, Hannah, helped him unhook and climb out of the harness. "What's going on?" he asked.

She shook her head. "You'd better see for yourself and decide," she said. "But I warn you—it's pretty grisly."

"You need to take a look at the guy in the passenger seat," Tony said.

It was grisly, all right, and Jake had to clench his jaw tight to maintain control as he looked at the man in the passenger seat of the van, his head almost severed from the neck. Jake forced himself to take his time and make as thorough an examination as possible, being careful not to disturb the scene, though the SAR personnel had probably already inadvertently destroyed evidence. Then again, the plummet off the road could have done that, too.

"I don't see anything that would cause a

wound like that accidentally," Tony said after Jake emerged from the van.

"No, I'd say that was done deliberately," Jake said. The wound had looked deep, made with a very sharp blade.

"Any idea who he is?" Ted asked. "We saw the uniform."

"Bernalillo County, New Mexico," Jake said. "His badge says Deputy Green. I'll have to contact them. The van isn't marked, but it has government plates."

"Huh," Tony said. "I didn't notice that."

"Have you looked in the back yet?" Jake nodded toward the rear of the vehicle.

"No. We thought we'd better wait for you."

The side door of the van was blocked, so Tony held back the driver's seat while Jake crawled inside. Then Tony played the beam of a powerful light over the back seat. "Looks like that seat belt's been cut," he said, spotlighting the cleanly cut edges of the safety belt.

Jake's foot nudged something and he looked down at a metal eye fixed into the floor of the vehicle. A short piece of chain was threaded through the eye, and beside the chain lay a pair of leg irons. A chill that had nothing to do with the ambient temperature ran up his spine as the meaning of that chain registered. He took the flashlight from his utility belt and began searching beneath the front seats. Something glinted, and he bent awkwardly and used a pen from his pocket to drag the item forward. "Are those handcuffs?" Tony asked.

"They're handcuffs." Jake backed out of the vehicle to find the rest of the SAR team around the opening, looking at him expectantly. "Looks like they were transporting a prisoner," he said.

"So the prisoner took advantage of the crash to get away," Tony said.

"Or the prisoner caused the crash when he made a break for it." Jake turned to Hannah. "Tell me everything you remember about the man you saw when you first got here. What did he look like?"

"He looked hurt," she said. "He had blood all over his head and his clothes."

"What was he wearing?"

She frowned. "I wasn't paying attention."

"Think. You saw something, even if you didn't consciously register the fact. It could be important."

She nodded, and closed her eyes. After a moment, she opened them again. "He was wearing a white jumpsuit. Or it had been white, before there was blood and mud all over it. But he didn't have a coat or hat. He's liable to freeze to death out here."

"Where's the closest place he could go for shelter?" Jake asked.

She looked around them, as if getting her bearings. "I don't know. We're twelve miles from town, over some pretty rugged terrain."

"There aren't any houses nearby," Tony said.

"What about the huts?" a tall, thin man asked.

"The huts?" Jake asked.

"There's a series of backcountry huts," the thin man said. "They're designed so backcountry skiers can spend the night. The huts are roughly a few hours on skis apart. They're not fancy, but there's a woodstove and firewood and bunks, some basic supplies in each one."

"How far is the nearest hut?" Jake asked.

The man scratched his chin. Unlike the other male SAR volunteers Jake had met, this man was clean-shaven. "A couple of hours? But that's with winter gear. It would be a lot tougher going in street clothes, without a coat or snowshoes or anything."

"So you're saying our guy would probably freeze to death before he got there?" Jake asked.

"Not necessarily," Tony said. "He's got to climb and all that strenuous activity would warm him up a lot. And it just depends on what kind of shape he's in and how determined he is. You'd be amazed what people can survive if they're stubborn enough. Sometimes that really is the only difference between making it out of an ordeal alive—some people just refuse to give up."

"I need to go after him," Jake said.

"That's our job," Tony said. "The search part of search and rescue."

"He's already killed one man," Jake said. "And I think he's probably armed. Deputy Green's weapon holster is empty. I can't let you go after him alone."

"Then you'll come with us." Tony looked around, then pointed to the thin man. "Danny, you've spent the most time on these trails. You come with us."

"I need to talk to the sheriff, see what he thinks," Jake said. "But Hannah should come, too." At her look of surprise, he added, "You're the only one of us who's seen this guy. That might prove useful."

She nodded. "We'll need the right equipment," she said. "Boots with crampons."

"Snowshoes, too," Danny said. "Skis would be good in places, but too hard to maneuver on the rough stuff unless you're really good. Like expert good."

"I can hold my own on skis, but I'm no mountaineering expert," Jake said.

Ted clapped him on the back. "You talk to the sheriff. Meanwhile, Hannah and Danny, go back to town and get the equipment you need. The rest of us will finish up here."

"We'll need to get forensics in here to photograph the scene and look for evidence, and you'll need the coroner," Jake said.

Ted nodded. "There's nothing we can do for either of the victims in this case, except stand by to help retrieve the bodies when the coroner is done." He looked up, squinting at the sky. "You'd better get a move on. We've only got a few hours before we start losing light."

DANNY MADE THE climb back up to the road first, then Hannah followed. "You okay going after this guy?" Danny asked as they waited for Jake to climb up.

She bristled. "Why wouldn't I be?" She didn't exactly relish the rough journey, but this was the kind of thing she had signed on for and trained for. And this man, even if he was a criminal and possibly a killer, was hurt and would need medical care.

Danny shrugged. "Just seems kind of dangerous."

She stared at him. "A lot of the stuff we do is dangerous." She waved her hand at the chasm below them. "This right here is dangerous."

"Nah, this is just a challenge. It's not dangerous if you know what you're doing."

She was saved having to argue with him by Jake's arrival. "Can you ride into town with me?" he asked. "We can stop by the sheriff's department, then you can help me round up the equipment I'll need."

"Sure." She appreciated that Jake didn't mind looking to her for help. She followed him to a sheriff's department SUV and waited while he shifted a pile of papers and gear from the passenger seat. She was scarcely buckled in when he swung the vehicle around and hit the siren for the drive back to town. As soon as they hit the city limits for Eagle Mountain, he ordered his phone to call the sheriff.

"What's up, Jake?" Sheriff Travis Walker sounded calm and easygoing, but Hannah knew he had a reputation as being no-nonsense. Her father had said that Travis was a man who worked more than he talked, and that had earned the young lawman the support of a lot of people in town.

Jake ran through the particulars of the crash, summing up with, "We've got a fugitive, probably armed, loose in the high country. He isn't dressed for the weather, so he'll probably head for the closest shelter, which is one of the back-country ski huts. I want to take a couple of the search and rescue team members up there to look for him."

"Who are you taking?" the sheriff asked.

"There's a guy, Danny, who's a local ski patroller. He knows the way to the closest hut. And the paramedic, Hannah. The man we're looking for was likely hurt in the accident, so he'll need medical attention. And she got a good look at him before he ran off, so she'll recognize him."

"I'm going to send Gage with you. He knows the area as well and you need another officer backing you up."

"Yes, sir."

"I'll track down Deputy Green's supervisor and get the particulars on our fugitive," Travis said. "I'll keep you posted."

Jake ended the call, and slowed the cruiser as they neared the center of town. He switched off the siren and glanced at Hannah. "Who can lend me the gear I'll need?"

"What size boots do you wear?" she asked.

"Thirteen."

"Then you can borrow my dad's stuff." She pointed ahead of them. "Turn left on Seventh Avenue and go all the way down to the Alpiner Inn."

The Alpiner was a two-story affair built to resemble a European chalet, with bright blue doors and shutters. In the spring, Hannah's mom filled the window boxes with red geraniums, but this time of year the boxes were mounded with snow. Jake pulled the SUV under the portico over the entrance and he and Hannah piled out.

The lobby was empty, so Hannah hit the bell on the front desk. Her mother, a petite woman with her riot of faded red curls tamed beneath a pink bandanna, bustled out of the back room. "Hannah?" She turned to Jake and took in his uniform. "Is something wrong?"

"Is Dad around? Deputy Gwynn needs to borrow some gear."

Her mom looked over her shoulder as Hannah's dad, Thad, came through the door. Despite his slightly bent frame and tonsure of white hair, his clear blue eyes and practically unlined face made him look younger than his sixty-two years. "Hello there." He smiled at Jake, a question in his eyes.

"Deputy Jake Gwynn." Jake stepped forward and offered his hand. "Your daughter said you had some winter gear I could borrow."

Thad shook Jake's hand. "Sure thing. Where are you headed?" he asked.

"There was a wreck on the highway up on Dixon Pass," Hannah said. "An injured man wandered off and we have to look for him. Jake needs some good climbing boots and warmer outerwear."

"But why is the deputy going along?" Thad asked.

Hannah looked to Jake. She had hoped to avoid alarming her parents, by making it seem that this was an ordinary rescue call. "We don't know this man's history and we have reason to believe he's armed," Jake said. "I'm going along as a precaution, but I'm new to the area, so I need to borrow some gear."

Thad nodded. "Come on back then."

They followed her dad through to the back of the building, where the family lived. "I heard the sheriff's department had a new hire," Thad said as he rummaged through his closet. "How do you like Eagle Mountain so far?"

"I'm very happy to be here," Jake said. "It's a beautiful place." He turned to study a display of medals and trophies next to the closet, many of them featuring images of climbers. "Are these all yours?"

Thad leaned out of the closet to see what had caught Jake's attention. "Yeah. I used to be a professional climber. I haven't competed in years, though I still keep my hand in, helping out with local clubs. Climbing is how I ended up in Eagle Mountain."

"I'm impressed," Jake said. There must have been two dozen awards in this case, in addition to several framed commendations.

Thad ducked back into the closet. "Have you spent much time in the backcountry?" he asked.

"Some," Jake said.

"You'll need these." Thad handed him a pair of stout leather boots, fitted with crampons.

"We need snowshoes, too," Hannah said.

Thad nodded, then looked Jake up and down. He dived back into the closet and came out again with a pair of insulated coveralls, patched at one knee with silver duct tape. "They're not pretty, but they're warm," he said. "What about a helmet?"

"I have one of those," Jake said. "We work enough rock slides and avalanches it's standard issue."

"What else then?"

"This should do it, Dad. Thanks." Hannah tugged at Jake's arm. "We're in a hurry." If they stayed, her father, who loved to talk, would start asking for more details, either about the accident, the man they were looking for or Jake himself.

Back in the lobby, Hannah said. "I'm going to get my gear. I'll meet you back outside."

She tried to slip past her parents, but her dad was watching for her. "This doesn't sound like an ordinary search and rescue mission," he said. "Who is this man you're looking for?"

"All I know is that he was in a car accident and he's hurt," she said. "He may be in shock and lost. I have to go help." She patted his shoulder. "Don't worry, Dad."

"Worrying is my job," Thad said. "It gets added to the job description the day your first child is born—you'll see."

She kissed his cheek. "I'll be fine," she said, then hurried up to her room before he could say more. She loved her parents, and loved that they were still close, but living at home at twenty-four did mean sacrificing a bit of privacy and independence. The pluses outweighed the minuses, but she sometimes envied those of her friends who had the luxury of keeping a few secrets from their folks.

When she returned to the SUV, Jake was hanging up the phone. "We know the fugitive's name is Charles Cutler—he goes by Charlie. He's thirty-seven, and he's a convicted murderer. He was serving time in New Mexico and was being transported to Junction for a trial for a murder in Colorado." he said. "The sheriff is trying to find out more. The deputy who was killed is Armando Green, twenty-eight, from Albuquerque, on the force for two years. The driver was a civilian, Geoffrey Calloway."

She piled her gear into the back on top of his, then slid into the passenger seat. "Those poor families," she said.

"Gage is going to meet us in the pullout near

the crash site," Jake said. He shifted the SUV into gear. "Cutler isn't some kid who made a rash mistake. He's a hardened killer. I don't think it's a good idea to involve civilians in this hunt."

"I'm not an ordinary civilian," she said. "Search and Rescue members are trained to work with law enforcement." Not that she had ever been in this kind of situation before, but she did have training. "I know how to stay out of the way and how to follow orders," she added.

He frowned but didn't say anything. He didn't use the siren on the way out of town this time. Hannah looked for some way to break the tension between them, but Jake spoke first. "Have you lived in Eagle Mountain long?" he asked after a moment.

"I grew up here. There at the inn. Where are you from?"

"Eastern Colorado. A little town called Haxtun."

"Sorry. I've never heard of it."

"Most people haven't. My parents have a ranch out there. They raise cattle and wheat."

"At least you're not a city boy."

"No, I'm not." His mouth twitched, as if he was amused.

She squirmed. "I just mean that if you grew up in a rural area, you probably know a little bit about dealing with the elements. They have big blizzards out there on the plains, don't they?"

"Oh yeah."

"And you really did handle the climbing well today. I've seen people freak out when they had to do something like that. It still scares me, even, and I've had hours and hours of training."

"I would have thought since your dad was a pro you would have been climbing since you were a kid," Jake said. "I saw all his trophies. He must be pretty good."

"I never had Dad's talent," she said. "I do it because it's part of my job. You looked like a natural, though."

"I was in good hands," he said. "I'm thinking it will be a little different up on the mountain."

"We'll be on trails part of the time," she said. "Trails with snow and ice, but that will make the going a little easier."

"First we need to see if we can pick up Cutler's trail. If he's still bleeding, that will help."

"If he's still bleeding, he may not get far," she said.

"Then that will be to our advantage."

She winced inwardly. Even though she knew the man they were searching for was a killer, the image of him, bleeding and terrified, was burned into her brain. All her training was devoted to helping people without judgment. She couldn't change her thinking now.

They neared the pullout and Jake slowed the SUV. Her Subaru was still there, along with another sheriff's department SUV. Sergeant Gage Walker, the sheriff's brother, got out of his vehicle as they pulled in behind him. A little taller and a little blonder than his brother, Gage was a friendly guy who often stopped by the inn to check on things or talk fishing with her dad.

"Hello, Hannah," Gage said. He came around to the back of Jake's SUV, where they were unloading their gear. "Danny's waiting for us at the trailhead on the other side of the waterfall. Did Travis tell you about this guy we're going after?"

"He said he killed three people."

"Uh-huh. Two women and a man." He glanced at Hannah, then away. "Pretty violent."

"He slit that deputy's throat and took his weapon," Jake said.

"Yeah, well, there's something else, something Travis just found out."

Jake and Hannah both stopped what they were doing and faced him. "What is it?" Hannah asked.

"Before Charlie Cutler was a killer, he was in the army. He went through the army's mountain-warfare school in upstate New York. That's summer and winter mountaineer training, rough terrain evacuation and mountain sniper training."

Jake swore under his breath.

"Right." Gage clapped him on the back. "We're about to go after a guy who's been trained to thrive in conditions most people couldn't even survive."

Chapter Three

They met up with Danny at the trailhead. Already the sun cast long shadows across the snow. In another hour they would be in full shadow, and an hour after that, twilight. Jake's heart raced with a sense of urgency. Hannah and Danny assured him they had trained for nighttime rescues, but darkness and colder temperatures made everything more difficult.

And this time they were going after a killer. Someone who could take advantage of the darkness to hide.

They started hiking up the trail, Danny leading the way, followed by Jake and Hannah, with Gage bringing up the rear. "It's going to take a couple of hours to reach the hut," Danny said. "We'll have a little more light after we cross the ridge into the valley where the hut sits, but we'll be coming back in the dark."

"Don't turn on your headlamps until we have to," Gage said. "If Cutler is up here, he'll be able to spot any lights approaching from a long way off and we don't want that."

"Right," Danny agreed. "Then we'd better hurry."

He set a swift pace up the steep path. No one said much, saving their breath for the climb. The narrow path wound up the mountain along a thin ridge, fields of pristine snow on either side, a canopy of blue overhead. If they hadn't been in search of a dangerous killer, Jake might have enjoyed the trek.

"It looks like this trail gets a lot of use," Jake said, as they neared the top of the first long switchback. The snow on the trail was packed down, with many boot prints, and slick ice in the sunny spots.

"This is the shortest route up to the huts and some really good skiing," Danny said. "And the avalanche danger is pretty low on this side, because the highway department regularly sets charges to release the snow to keep the road clear."

"Makes it harder to track our fugitive, though," Gage said.

"We don't even know Cutler came this way," Hannah said.

"It's the easiest route up the mountain, so he's an idiot if he didn't head this way," Danny said.

"Except he has to know someone would come after him," Hannah said.

"I don't see any tracks off the trail," Gage said.

"Would he have known about the huts?" Hannah asked.

"There's a sign at the trailhead," Danny said. "If he saw that, he'd have known this was his best bet for shelter. He'd want to get there before nightfall."

"What if someone else is already at the hut?" she asked.

"I hope they aren't," Gage said. "For their sake."

Hannah's stricken expression told Jake she understood that Cutler was likely to kill anyone who got in his way. That included all of them.

About five hundred yards up the first steep incline, Danny stopped and pointed to the ground at their feet. "I think that's blood," he said.

Jake knelt and examined the drops, bright red where they had frozen on the snow. "This looks pretty fresh," he said.

"It could be an injured animal," Gage said.

"Maybe." Jake straightened and stared up the slope. "But I don't think so."

"Yeah, I don't think so, either," Gage said. They started out hiking again. Danny quickened the pace, moving just below a trot. The altimeter on Jake's watch showed just over ten thousand feet and he could definitely feel it, breathing hard, his heart pounding. He told himself that Cutler, who had been in a prison in Albuquerque, would be at a greater disadvantage, living at a lower altitude.

At the top of the next switchback, they met two men hiking down, skis strapped to their big packs. "Have you passed anyone on your way down?" Jake asked.

"Nobody," the older of the two, with a full red beard, said.

"You're starting up kind of late," his friend said.

"Were you at the hut?" Jake asked.

"We passed by there," the bearded man said. "It didn't look like there was anyone there, so you should have the place to yourselves."

"Thanks," Jake said, and they moved on. At the top of the next switchback, Jake motioned for Hannah to move past him, and he dropped back to speak to Gage. "What do you think?" he asked.

"I think if we get there before him, we can hide and take him easier," Gage said.

"Right. But if he was ahead of us, and those two didn't see him, where did he go? We're above tree line and there aren't a lot of places to hide around here. We spotted those two long before we met up with them."

"I don't know," Gage admitted. "I haven't seen any place where anyone has gone off trail, but maybe they teach things in that army course that we don't know about. They must have stuff in their training about evading the enemy."

"They probably taught him how to sneak up and ambush someone from behind, too," Jake said, keeping his voice low so Hannah and Danny wouldn't hear.

Gage grimaced. "And we're pretty exposed up here on this ridge."

"I'd feel better if we didn't have civilians with us," Jake said.

"I've worked with Search and Rescue before," Gage said. "They've got solid training and they know how to follow orders. Don't worry about them."

What some people called worry was Jake's idea of being prepared for the worst. But he merely nodded and moved up alongside Hannah again. "How are you doing?" he asked.

"I'd be enjoying myself if we were doing this for some other reason." She flashed him a smile. "It's beautiful up here."

"It is." Except those clear skies and open snow fields made him feel like a target. Still, he reminded himself, as far as they knew, Cutler only had a pistol. He'd have to get pretty close in order to fire on them. "Thanks for agreeing to come with us," he said.

"If you find Mr. Cutler, you'll need me," she said.

He hoped that was the only reason they needed her. A man who would cut the throat of a sheriff's deputy the way Cutler had wouldn't hesitate to kill anyone else he thought was in his way.

HANNAH KEPT HER eyes on the ground, searching for more spots of blood alongside the trail. Those first spots had been so vivid, a scattering of bright red against the stark white. But they hadn't seen any more. Was it because Cutler had staunched the flow, or because he had left the trail at some point and struck out in some other direction?

They only had another hour or so before the sun set behind the mountains, which meant that no matter what they found, they'd be descending in the dark. She had hiked with a headlamp before, but coming down would be a lot colder. It was cold enough now, the tips of her fingers, even in insulated mittens, going numb periodically, until she shoved them deep into the pockets of her parka to thaw, and her cheeks stinging. She told herself as long as she could feel them she didn't need to worry about frost-bite. Coming down, they would be a lot more fatigued, too. It was the kind of conditions that were ripe for mistakes.

When she lifted her gaze from the trail, her view was of Jake Gwynn's back. For a flat-lander, he was handling the climbing well. Un-like her, he wasn't focused on the trail. Instead, he constantly scanned the area around them, his attitude alert. While she knew, objectively, that Charlie Cutler was dangerous, Jake accepted it as fact. He was probably used to expecting the worst from people, while her training was to seek out the best in everyone. That dissonance between what the facts told her and what she wanted to believe added to the unreal quality of this whole afternoon.

Up ahead, Danny stopped and waited for the rest of them to catch up. "The hut is just over this next ridge," he said. "About another half mile."

"Can you see this trail from the hut?" Jake asked.

"No. The hut sits in a little depression, in a sheltered area. If you're inside, you really can't see anyone until they're up on you. There aren't many windows, in any case, which makes it easier to heat."

"If Cutler is in there and has built a fire, we'll

be able to see the smoke," Hannah said. "We'll probably smell it before we see it."

"He'll know we're likely to come after him," Gage said. "So he might not light a fire. If I remember, there are supplies in the huts, right?"

"Yeah," Danny said. "Water and firewood, but also some blankets, first aid and emergency supplies, and some canned food."

"All right," Gage said. "When we get within sight of the hut, you and Hannah need to fall back. We'll stop and observe for a while, then Jake and I will move forward."

Hannah and Danny nodded.

They started out again, a new silence enveloping them, as without discussion they tried to make as little noise as possible. Twenty-five minutes later they reached the top of the ridge, and stopped to look down on the hut, a simple A-frame painted a soft gray that blended with the shadows of the ridge above. Firewood filled a separate woodshed a few feet from the door, and an outhouse painted to match the hut itself sat twenty yards from the back door.

Danny sniffed the air. "No smoke."

Jake pulled a pair of binoculars from his pack and focused on the hut. "There are footprints leading to the doors, front and back," he said, his voice very low.

"Could be from other visitors," Gage said. "A lot of people use these huts."

Jake stowed the binoculars. "I'll go down first," he said.

"Better strap on snowshoes," Danny said. He swept his hand toward the expanse of snow between the trail and the cabin. "That snow is feet deep. Follow the ski trail in—it will be more packed."

Jake nodded and slipped the pack from his back to unstrap the snowshoes. He removed his crampons and stepped into the snowshoes, then bent to tighten them, his gaze focused on the cabin, which was still and silent.

"I'll cover you." Gage unholstered his weapon. "You two get down," he said to Danny and Hannah.

The sight of his drawn pistol made the danger seem so much more real, and she fought back a sickening wave of fear. She sat in the snow, pulling her knees to her chest, as Jake started down toward the hut. She wished she could see what he was doing. Then again, she didn't really want to see if Cutler shot him. She closed her eyes. The saying in SAR was you never knew what you'd find when you went out on a call, but she couldn't at her most imaginative have anticipated a day like today.

"Hey, it'll be all right." Danny moved closer and put his arm around her.

She shoved him away and glared.

He drew back. "You don't have to be so touchy."

And he didn't have to try to take advantage of the situation. She didn't need him to "comfort" her, thank you very much.

"What's going on down there?" Danny asked Gage.

"Jake is almost to the hut."

That was a good sign, wasn't it? Unless Cutler wanted Jake closer before he killed him.

Another long wait. Hannah focused on taking deep breaths, counting with each one. One… two….three…four…

"He's motioned for us to come on down." Gage stood and holstered his weapon.

Hannah rose, staggering a little on frozen feet, and joined the other two in fumbling into snowshoes. They started down to the hut, sinking five or six inches before finding a good footing. Anyone who came along would spot their trail from a mile away.

The whole area was in full shadow now, blue in the dwindling light. Jake came partway up the trail to meet them. "If he was here, he's gone now," he said. "The place is empty. We should stop and get warm, maybe eat something before we head back down."

"It's getting too dark to track him now," Gage said. "But if we can determine which way he headed, it will give us a head start tomorrow. We can probably get a helicopter up here to help out."

They walked spread out across the snow, headed toward the hut. The idea of a hot drink and a chance to sit down for a while sent a burst of energy through her. Another few hours and this would all be over and—

Before she could finish the thought, something whistled past her. Then a body slammed into hers. She sank into the snow, the breath knocked out of her, then realized the sounds around her were shots. Jake lay sprawled on top of her. "Are you okay?" she asked, trying to throw off his weight enough to sit up.

"Stay down," he ordered, and rolled over enough to draw his weapon, just as another bullet struck near them, snow flying up where it struck like feathers from a burst pillow. The sound it made was soft, almost gentle, in sharp contrast with the fear that gripped her. Were they going to die here, slaughtered like animals in the midst of so much beauty?

Chapter Four

Jake fired in the direction the shots had come, the report of his weapon loud and echoing, overlapping a similar report from Gage's gun. Their fire wasn't returned, so he lowered his gun and listened. His own ragged breathing filled his ears, then Hannah whimpered and squirmed beneath him. "I can't breathe," she whispered. "Could you get off of me?"

He hadn't even realized he was still sprawled on top of her. When the first shot had rang out, he had acted on instinct, pushing her down and shielding her. Now he knelt beside her, knees sinking in the snow, snowshoes kicked up awkwardly behind him. "Are you okay?"

"I'm okay." She raised herself to all fours and looked toward the hut. "Is he in there?"

"I don't think so. Not anymore."

Gage crawled over to them. "I think he was firing from behind the outhouse," he said. "But he's gone now. I can just about make out his tracks headed away from there."

Jake pulled the binoculars from his pack and focused on the outhouse, then shook his head. "The light's too bad to make out anything." He lowered the glasses and stared down the slope. "Do we go after him, or head back?"

"If we could get inside for a bit, drink some water and have something to eat, we'll do better on the trip down," Hannah said. "And we might be able to tell if he took any supplies from the hut when he left."

"She's got a good point," Gage said. He stood and offered a hand to Hannah. "Let's go down."

Jake's pulse hammered in his ears all the way down to the hut, and by the time they reached the door he ached from holding himself so rigid. But no further shots rang out. Gage led them in a wide arc around the steps in front of the hut. The door stood partly open, as if Cutler had exited in a hurry.

The inside of the hut was as cold as it had been outside. Danny switched on his headlamp, and Jake took a flashlight from his belt and played the beam across the interior, revealing a single room with a woodstove against the back wall, a table and chairs in front of the stove and triple bunks on either side wall. A single cabinet on the back wall to the left of the stovepipe stood open, the contents tumbling out. "Looks like he rifled through here," Gage said.

"He used the first aid kit." Hannah moved to the table, her headlamp spotlighting a tangle of bloody gauze, unwound bandage and an open tube of antibiotic cream. She frowned at the disarray. "I can't really tell much about the nature of the wounds from this. He was bleeding— maybe from broken glass from the wreckage?"

She reached out toward the roll of bandaging but Jake caught and held her hand. "Don't touch anything more than necessary," he said.

She nodded and he released her and stepped back.

Danny moved to a wooden locker at the end of one set of bunks. Gingerly, using only one finger, he raised the lid. "He's been in here," he said. "There was a pack in here with more first aid and emergency supplies missing."

"You're sure?" Jake moved in beside him.

"We stocked all the huts at the beginning of the season," Danny said. "The packs are designed so that in an emergency, someone could carry what they need to someone who was hurt on the ski trails."

"What did the pack contain?" Gage asked.

"Basic first aid supplies—bandages, a splint and instant ice packs." Danny tilted his head, considering. "There were a couple of emergency blankets—those foil-looking things that utilize the body's own heat for warmth. Some chemical heat packs and emergency food—energy gels and bars. Extra socks and gloves and a hat." He peered into the locker again. "I think last time I was up here someone had left one of those big wool Nordic sweaters in here, too. That's gone."

"So he has a pack, warmer clothing, food and first aid supplies," Gage said. "He's in a lot better shape that he was when he left the van a few hours ago."

"He must have taken the deputy's rifle with him when he left the van too," Jake said. "I didn't think about that at the time, but that wasn't a pistol he was firing at us."

"We'll have to contact the Bernalillo County Sheriff's Department and find out what kind of weapon Green would have had, and how much ammunition," Gage said.

"My guess is Cutler has plenty left," Jake said. "He didn't fire that many shots."

"He just wanted to buy time to get away," Gage said. "We'll need to close this area to the public until we find him."

"Good luck with that," Danny said.

"What do you mean?" Jake asked.

"I mean there are probably ten trails that access this basin," Danny said. "You don't have the personnel to station someone at every trailhead. You can post signs, but people will ignore them. It happens every fire season. The forest rangers spend a lot of time running people out of closed areas. It's always the same story. 'I didn't see the sign' or even 'I didn't think one or two people would be a problem.' There are always people who think the rules don't apply to them."

"Maybe if the signs say a killer is on the loose, people will take them seriously," Jake said.

"You can try," Danny said. "But I wouldn't count on it."

"We need to eat and get warm before we head back down," Hannah said. "I know we're not supposed to touch anything, but we're not going to make it down safely if we don't get some fuel in us."

"Go ahead," Gage said. "We're not going to find anything here that tells us where Cutler is headed or what his plans are."

Hannah moved to the gas cooktop and picked up the kettle. "I'm going to get some snow to melt for water for coffee," she said. "Danny, can you fix something for us to eat?"

"I'll go out with you," Jake said. He moved with her toward the cabin's back door. "Let me go out first. Just in case Cutler is still out there."

Her eyes widened, but she said nothing, only

nodded and stepped back, cradling the empty kettle under one arm, her snowshoes under the other.

He slipped outside, snowshoes in hand, and waited in the shadow of the hut, ears straining to hear anything but his own breathing. After a long moment, he looked back toward Hannah and nodded. "Switch off your light," he said, keeping his voice low.

She did as he asked and he moved closer so she'd be sure to hear him. "Can you see well enough to move around without a light?"

"Yes." She bent and began strapping on her snowshoes.

He put on his own snowshoes and took a few steps away from the hut, braced for the impact of a bullet. Yes, he had on a ballistics vest underneath the insulated coveralls, but he didn't have faith the vest would make much difference to a slug from a high-powered rifle.

Nothing happened. Quiet wrapped itself around him, and he wondered if this was what sudden deafness was like. He looked up at the first stars shining out from the canopy of blackness, like pinholes punctured in a blackout curtain.

Hannah moved up alongside him. "We need to get a ways from the hut," she said. "To be sure the snow is clean."

"All right."

Moving in the dark was awkward, but they made it about a hundred yards before she stopped and scooped the kettle into the snow. Then she turned and hurried back to the hut, so that he had to jog to keep up with her, snow-shoes making muffled slapping sounds against the powdery snow.

Back inside, someone had started a fire in the woodstove. Danny had placed a cutting board on one of the bottom bunks and was slicing summer sausage and cheese. Gage had pulled one of the chairs from the table over to the stove and sat in it, reloading his pistol.

"Your perp took all the chocolate," Danny said. "This is all from my pack. There's crackers and dried mango, too." He indicated a couple of plastic bags beside the cutting board.

"There's still coffee in here." Hannah took a plastic container of grounds from the single cabinet.

They ate quickly, then Hannah and Danny cleared up the remains of their meal. "Before we go, I want to see if we can figure out which way Cutler headed," Jake said. "It will give us a head start when we pick up the search again in the morning."

"Good idea," Gage said. He stood and began

pulling on his parka. "You two wait and we'll head back down together," he told Danny.

Jake pulled on his borrowed parka and a balaclava, then strapped the helmet on over that. At the back door, he and Gage put on their snowshoes, and set off toward the outhouse. Ten steps from the doorway, darkness closed around them. He had a moment of vertigo, suspended between the soft snow and the stinging cold of the night air. "You think Cutler is still out here?" Gage asked.

"Why would he still be here?" Jake asked.

"Maybe waiting for us to leave? He could spend the night in the hut."

"He's bound to know we'll keep looking for him. And we'll start the last place we saw him—here." Jake shook his head. "I think he's on his way to the next hut."

"Then we'll start one search team there at first light," Gage said. His footsteps crunched softly on the snow. "Come on. Let's see if we can find any sign of him."

As Gage and Jake exited out the back door, Hannah dropped into the chair by the fire that Gage had vacated and sipped the last of the coffee. Danny pulled a second chair alongside her. "Wild day, huh?" he said.

"All I want to do is get home," she said. Even

the thought of having to hike in the darkness back down to her car exhausted her.

"Finding that deputy this morning was rough," Danny said. "Don't let it get to you."

"I won't." She hadn't even been thinking about Deputy Green, as terrible as that was. He wasn't, unfortunately, the first dead person she had seen working Search and Rescue.

"What do you think of the new cop?" Danny asked.

"He's okay." She stared into the fire, aware of Danny watching her. "He's not a whiner."

"Maybe he'll last longer than some of the others. Seems like we've gone through a lot of deputies in the past few years."

"You know what it's like in small towns," she said. "People come here to get experience, then move on to some place that pays better or is less expensive to live—or both. It happens everywhere, not just the sheriff's department." One of the reasons she continued to live at the Alpiner with her parents was that it was so hard to find dependable employees who would stay on the job. She worked three twelve-hour shifts a week as a paramedic and had the other four days off to help at the inn.

"He seems pretty into you," Danny said.

She frowned. "You're imagining things."

"I didn't imagine the way he threw himself on

you when the bullets started flying. I was standing just as close and he didn't try to save me."

"Are you jealous?" she asked.

He said something obscene.

Fortunately, he didn't have time to pick up the discussion. The back door opened and Jake and Gage stepped in, stamping their snowshoes on the rubber door mat. "Did you find anything?" Danny asked.

Gage pushed back the hood of his parka and shook his head. "It's too dark to tell much of anything. There are tracks over behind the outhouse, but no way to tell much. We'll be back up at first light tomorrow with a search team."

"If you need help, I'm up for it," Danny said.

"Thanks," Gage said. "But this will be all law enforcement personnel."

"Yeah, I guess with a cop dead, it will be an all-out manhunt," Danny said.

"We want to make sure he doesn't kill anyone else," Jake said. "How far is it from here to the next hut in line?"

"Five miles," Danny said.

"Is that the closest shelter?" Jake asked.

"Pretty much," Danny said.

"There are some mine ruins not far from that hut," Hannah said. "Some of the buildings aren't in bad shape. He might try to hide there. Less chance of running into other people, at least this time of year."

"What about transportation out of here?" Jake asked.

"Other than going back down to the highway or into town—he could hijack a vehicle at a trailhead," Gage said.

"He could hike over the ridge into the town of Paradise," Danny said. "It's not the easiest route, but it's not impossible. From there he could go just about anywhere."

"Is there a path or a road he'd follow to do that?" Jake asked.

"There's an old Jeep road," Danny said. "It's closed this time of year, but if he's motivated enough…" He shrugged.

"I think he's motivated," Gage said. He looked around the cabin. "Let's get out of here."

They headed out, changing out of their snowshoes when they reached the trail. Hannah's headlamp cast a trembling blue circle of light in front of her and cold seeped through the layers of her clothing, until she could no longer feel her fingers and her teeth chattered. She forced herself to move faster, trying to generate warmth. But as they moved around a ridge and into the open, the wind buffeted them, sending her staggering sideways.

Jake caught and steadied her. "Careful," he said. "It's really icy here."

She leaned into him an extra moment, grateful for his steadiness—and for the way he blocked her from the wind. Ha! Danny thought Jake was attracted to her. Maybe he merely appreciated her usefulness as a windbreak, too.

She set out walking again and Jake stayed close behind her. "What do you remember about Cutler's injuries?" he asked.

So this was what they were going to talk about. So much for having any chance to relax and forget why they were up here. "He was bleeding from the head," she said, forcing herself to recall the image of the man standing at the edge of the ravine. "His clothes were covered in blood. A lot of it. And there was blood running down his face. But even minor head wounds can bleed a great deal, so it's possible this was just minor lacerations. Still, I got the impression he was in pain. And…and frightened." That moment when their eyes met, it had been like looking into the eyes of an injured animal. Or a child. The look was one she had seen in other victims—sometimes it was the last thing she saw before the light faded and life ebbed away.

She shrugged her shoulders, shaking off the thought. Cutler might have been frightened, but he was upright and moving and far from death. The fact that he had made it to the hut despite his lack of winter clothing spoke to his stamina and fortitude—or, as Gage had said, desperation. "Was he…was he facing the death penalty?" she asked.

"New Mexico and Colorado don't have the death penalty anymore," Jake said. "But I imagine he was looking at spending the rest of his life behind bars."

She shoved both hands in the pockets of her parka and hunched against the wind. The prospect of permanently losing his freedom might make a person take all kinds of crazy risks.

"He's in bigger trouble now," Jake said. "He killed Deputy Green, and the driver probably died because of Cutler's actions. Don't feel sorry for him."

"I don't," she said. Not when she thought about Deputy Green and the driver. Her head ached from fatigue and cold and altitude, and maybe from trying to make sense of a fragmented picture she was only able to see in bits and pieces. Charlie Cutler was an injured man and she was supposed to help injured people. He was also a multiple murderer who wasn't likely to show her any mercy if they met up again.

She lifted her head and tried to see into the blackness beyond the circle of her headlamp.

Was Cutler out there in that cold darkness? Was he watching them, even now? If so, what was he thinking? Would the answer to that question make her even more afraid?

Chapter Five

Hannah had agreed to work the front desk of the inn the next morning, so she reluctantly hauled herself out of bed and made it downstairs in time to handle checkout for two couples who were departing that day. She was finishing up their paperwork when her mom, Brit, emerged from the back room, coffee mug in hand. She slid the coffee toward Hannah. "I thought you could use this."

"Thanks." Hannah wrapped both hands around the mug and drank deeply of the coffee laced with sugar and heavy cream. Her mother wasn't a believer in skim anything.

"Did you find the man you were looking for?" Brit asked.

Hannah shook her head. "No. The sheriff's department is going out to look more this morning."

"I heard a helicopter fly over a few minutes ago and wondered," Brit said. She settled onto a stool behind the counter. A trim woman dressed in leggings and a lace-trimmed tunic, Brit Richards still had the smooth, creamy complexion of a much younger woman. Only the fine lines fanning out from her blue eyes and the streaks of white in her fading red hair betrayed her as slightly north of fifty. "I'm glad you're not going this time. I don't like to think of you anywhere near a murderer."

Hannah set down her coffee and faced her mom. "How did you know the man is a murderer?"

"Ashley stopped by last night after you left to tell us about the Bernalillo County sheriff's deputy who was killed. She said the killer was loose somewhere near Dixon Pass." Ashley Gray was one of her mom's best friends and worked for the city—right next door to the sheriff's department. "She didn't know you were searching with them, or I'm sure she wouldn't have told me," Brit added.

Hannah sighed. News like this wouldn't have remained a secret for long. Any number of people regularly monitored the emergency channels online and passed along the latest news about police and fire calls. "The man they're looking for was injured in the car accident," Hannah said. "Danny and I went along to take care of him if he was found."

"I don't see why they had to take both of you," Brit said.

"Danny was guiding them to the ski hut, and I... I was actually the only person who saw this man," Hannah said. "The sheriff's deputies thought it would be a good idea to have me identify him."

"But they don't need you to identify him today?"

"I guess not." Hannah had a feeling the shots Charlie Cutler had fired on them had persuaded the sheriff's department not to involve Search and Rescue any further. "I'm sure the paramedics on call today are standing by in case they're needed." Part of her wished she was on the schedule today, though she had decidedly mixed feelings about facing Charlie Cutler again.

"Deputy Gwynn seemed very nice," Brit said.

"Yes," Hannah said, bracing herself for what she suspected was coming.

"Good-looking, too. About your age. Is he single?"

"Mom." Hannah tried to put a warning in the single syllable, which Brit ignored.

"I know it's not easy to meet eligible men in a small community," Brit said. "It's always interesting when someone new moves in. I imagine he'll get a lot of interest."

"I'm sure he'll have his pick of people to date," Hannah said.

"You never know, dear. I wasn't interested in getting married at all when I met your father."

"I know, Mom." She knew all about her parents' meet-cute when he collapsed a tower of canned goods in the grocery store where her mother was working a summer job between semesters of college. As they picked up cans together, her dad asked her out. Her mom said no. He came by every day after that, waited in her checkout line to buy a pack of gum and eventually persuaded her to go out with him. Two months later, they were married. It was a crazy, romantic story, and one Hannah thought was very unlikely to happen to her. For one thing, meeting at the scene of an accident involving a violent killer definitely didn't qualify as a meet-cute.

She was saved from having to explain this by the ringing phone. "Alpiner Inn," she answered. "This is Hannah. How may I help you?"

"Hannah, it's Jake. Deputy Gwynn."

"Good morning, Deputy," she said, aware of her mother watching her. "Is the search over already?"

"Not yet. No sign of him at the second hut."

Her stomach tightened. So Charlie Cutler was still at large. Was he even alive? He wouldn't be the first person to freeze to death in the mountains in winter. If he was still alive, what would happen when the searchers cornered him?

"The helicopter is searching the area now," Jake continued. "And some of us are getting ready to head out again. I called because I need to get your statement about yesterday."

"My statement?"

"We need a formal statement of everything you saw at the crash site. For the case file."

"Oh, of course. Do you want to do that now? Over the phone?"

"No. Could you meet me at the sheriff's department this afternoon? Would two o'clock work for you?"

Hannah turned to her mom. "I need to go to the sheriff's department at two to give a statement about what happened yesterday," she said.

"That will be fine," Brit said. "Tell Deputy Gwynn I said hello."

"I can be there," Hannah said.

"Great. If anything changes, I'll let you know."

She hung up the phone and turned to find her mother smiling. "Wear that new blue sweater this afternoon," Brit said. "It's a great color on you."

"Mom. This is serious police business. I'm not trying to impress anyone."

"Well, you don't want to show up in a stained sweatshirt, do you?"

Hannah looked down at the sweatshirt, which advertised a local outdoor guide service. She hadn't noticed the yellowish blotch across her stomach when she had grabbed it this morning. "I'll go change," she said.

"The blue sweater," her mother said.

Hannah stomped up the stairs to her room. The inn had an elevator, but she seldom used it, preferring the workout from the stairs. She unlocked her door and walked to her closet, determined to find anything to wear but the blue sweater, but after discarding half a dozen choices, ended up with the sweater anyway. It was a personal favorite—soft and well fitting, and comforting. Wearing it made her feel good, and she needed all the confidence she could get if she was going to be giving an official statement to law enforcement. Even though she hadn't done anything wrong, it still felt intimidating.

Her mother nodded in approval when Hannah returned to the front desk, then left to talk to their housekeeper, Jade. Hannah spent the rest of the morning answering the phone, steering guests toward good places for lunch and trying not to brood over Charlie Cutler, Jake Gwynn and the aftermath of what had seemed yesterday like a routine call for a traffic accident.

At two o'clock she walked into the lobby of the Rayford County Sheriff's Department. Though she had walked past the building hundreds of times, on her way to one of the shops in downtown Eagle Mountain, she had never been inside. The lobby was small and utilitarian, the walls painted gray and lined with photographs of officers past and present, in and out of uniform. A portrait of the sheriff, Travis Walker, was centered on the right-hand wall, one she recognized from his campaign posters. Tall, dark and handsome pretty much summed up the thirty-something sheriff, who had a good reputation in the community.

"You must be Hannah Richards." The woman who had emerged from a door to Hannah's left was old enough to have a complete head of white hair and a network of fine lines around her mouth and eyes. She wore blue-framed glasses and large blue hoop earrings. "I'll let Deputy Gwynn know you're here."

The woman moved to the desk at the back of the room and Hannah continued to study the pictures. She hadn't located one of Jake—maybe he was too new to the department. "Thanks for coming, Hannah."

She turned to find the man himself, his face

slightly windburned and hair ruffled, but looking more alert and rested than she felt. "Come back here and we'll get this over with," Jake said, and held a door open for her.

She followed him down a hallway to a small, gray room outfitted with a single table and three chairs. "I need to record your statement and that will be easier in here," Jake said as he ushered her into the room. "Can I get you anything? Some water?"

"No, I'm fine." She pulled out one of the chairs and sat, while he settled opposite her and pulled forward a file folder. "Did you find any sign of Cutler yet?" she asked.

"No. He's not in any of the obvious places we thought he might seek shelter, but there's a lot of territory to cover out there. A lot of places to hide."

She nodded. "I guess so."

"We'll continue to hunt for him, and we're posting signs at all the trailheads warning people to be on the lookout for him, and not to confront him if they do see him. Maybe someone will spot him and contact us."

"I hope so."

He opened the folder. "Thanks for coming this afternoon. I'm going to start the recording." He hit a remote, then recited his name, her name and the date and time. Then he began laying out some photos in front of her. "Can you tell me if any of these pictures are of the man you saw at the accident scene yesterday?"

She leaned forward and studied the photographs. They were all of very similar men—white, mid to late thirties, with close-cropped hair. The thought flashed through her mind that she might not be able to identify the man she had seen. After all, they had only stared at each other for a few seconds, and he had been bleeding…then she came to the last photograph in the row and recognition jolted her. "That's him," she said, pointing to the photo.

"You're sure?" Jake asked.

She nodded. "The eyes, and that gap in his eyebrow." She indicated the space on the photo. "I hadn't really thought about it before, but as soon as I saw this picture, I knew it was him." In the black-and-white photo, Charlie Cutler faced the camera, unsmiling. He was better looking than she remembered, handsome even, in an unpolished way, clean-shaven and clear-eyed, with broad shoulders and erect posture. "He looks like a soldier, doesn't he?" she asked, recalling what Gage had said about Cutler's military background.

"Not just any soldier," Jake said. "I did a little reading this morning about the army's mountain-warfare school. The school has its origins in the Tenth Mountain Division that trained on the Continental Divide here in Colorado during World War II. The training includes winter survival and maneuvering in really rugged conditions. The people who complete that training are in a pretty elite group."

She shuddered, not wanting to think about the advantages that kind of training would give a killer.

Jake picked up the photo of Cutler and stacked it on top of the others and returned them to the file folder. "Tell me everything you remember about yesterday at the accident scene," he said.

She began with the callout. "The dispatcher said a motorist had reported seeing a boxy white van go off the road near the pullout for the falls," she said. "I was shopping at that end of town, so I drove up there. I must have been the closest, because I arrived first. I got out and looked things over. I could see the van below, and I called down and listened for an answer. If someone was alive, I wanted them to know help was on the way."

"When did you see Cutler?" Jake asked.

"I heard him first. Feet slipping on loose rock—like someone climbing up. Which in itself was pretty incredible. It's very steep there. We had to use ropes to get down. Yet he climbed up that snowy, muddy slope under his own power. And injured."

"So you heard him. Then what?"

"I turned toward the sound. He was standing there, just…looking at me. He had blood on his shirt and running down his face, and his clothes were very muddy. I said something to him—I think I introduced myself and asked his name. I'm sure I said I wanted to help. Then you arrived and I turned toward you—when I looked back, he was gone." She frowned. "You didn't see him?"

Jake shook his head. "I had just gotten out of my car and was focused on you. I couldn't see the edge of the ravine from where I was standing."

She nodded. "That's really everything. I probably looked at him for ten seconds or less."

"And you think he came from the wrecked van?"

"Yes. I'm sure he climbed up from there. The mud all over him and the blood—I couldn't see any major injury, so I think maybe it was from broken glass." She frowned. "He would have been in the back seat of the van, in leg irons and handcuffs, though maybe he managed to get free of those and kill the deputy… Is that what caused the accident, do you think?"

"We're still trying to put the pieces together.

Is there anything else you can tell us about your encounter with Charlie Cutler?"

"As a paramedic, my first assessment was that he was in shock. He looked dazed, and with the cold and all that blood, it would be a natural reaction. But then, he'd made the climb up the slope, and that would take a lot of physical strength. And he looked...frightened." She bit her lip. "You'd think I would be the one to feel threatened by him, but really, he looked harmless. A little lost."

"He probably was frightened," Jake said. "He could have been killed in the wreck, and he'd just murdered a sheriff's deputy. He had to know if he was caught he'd be severely punished. He probably saw me and my uniform and that's why he ran." His eyes met hers, dark with concern. "I know to you he was a hurt, scared victim whom you were there to help. But Charlie Cutler is definitely not harmless. Don't make the mistake of thinking that."

She nodded. His words sent an icy shard of fear through her. "Can you tell me about the murders he was convicted of? Gage said two women and one man?"

"The woman was a bank teller. He attacked her outside her apartment building one night. The man and the woman were a couple he at-

tacked in a park one evening a month later."
Jake's jaw tightened, lips compressed and pale.

"Is there something else?" she asked. "Something you aren't telling me?" She leaned toward him across the table. "I want to know. I'm not going to freak out, I promise."

He exhaled a long breath, then reached over and switched off the recording. "This doesn't go any further than this room," he said.

She nodded. "I promise I won't tell a soul."

"Cutler was convicted of killing the three people I mentioned, but he's a suspect for five other murders, at least. He was being transported to Junction to be tried in one of those cases. All women." He swallowed, Adam's apple bobbing, then met and held her gaze. "The Bernalillo County Sheriff's Department sent over a file, with photographs of his suspected victims. All women in their twenties and thirties, athletic builds, with blue eyes and reddish hair."

She drew a sharp breath. The women he had described... "They all look like me," she whispered.

Chapter Six

"The search for escaped murderer Charles 'Charlie' Cutler continues in the rugged San Juan Mountains outside Eagle Mountain, Colorado. Cutler escaped custody four days ago after killing a Bernalillo County, New Mexico, sheriff's deputy while being transported for a new trial in Junction, Colorado. After stealing survival gear and supplies from a remote cabin, Cutler, who is reported to be suffering unspecified injuries, has vanished in a rugged, mostly roadless area where temperatures have hovered near zero every night. When asked whether he believed Cutler was still alive, Rayford County Sheriff Travis Walker stated authorities are approaching the search as if Cutler is still at large. The sheriff emphasized that anyone who thinks they have seen Cutler should contact local law enforcement and not attempt to approach, as he is known to be armed and is considered very dangerous."

Tony reached up and switched off the radio that sat on a high shelf in the Search and Rescue headquarters, sandwiched between a stack of report binders and a CPR practice dummy dressed in a pink-and-green floral aloha shirt. Most of the other two dozen members of the teams occupied various seating in the converted garage space that served as meeting room and training center, from folding chairs that creaked every time someone shifted their weight to a sagging plaid sofa Danny had found on the side of the road and hauled into the building. He sat at one end of the decrepit piece of furniture now, the other cushions occupied by Sheri and Ted.

The monthly training meetings were mandatory for SAR volunteers and included a regular mixture of bad coffee, griping, gossip and actual education. "Cutler's dead," Danny said as soon as the radio fell silent. "Some hiker will stumble on his body this spring."

"Some people don't turn up for years," Ted said. "Remember that body retrieval we did in Galloway Basin two summers ago? That woman had been missing for eight years."

"I heard Cutler was like, ex–Special Forces or something." The speaker was the newest member of the group, trainee Austen Morrissey, a baby-faced thirty-year-old with thinning brown hair and wire-rimmed glasses.

"Someone like that could survive a long time in the wilderness."

"Sure, in the summer, if he could forage food and steal from tourists," Danny said. "Those granola bars he stole from the ski hut aren't going to get him very far."

"There are a lot of summer cabins off those Jeep roads up there," Ted said. "He could break into one of them and help himself and no one would know until the owners come back in June."

"What do you think, Hannah?" Danny asked.

Hannah had been trying to ignore the conversation about Charlie Cutler. She didn't want to think about him at all, though the memory of him staring at her, blood streaming down his face, would pop into her head at the oddest moments—when she was almost asleep, or when she was driving and let her mind wander. "I don't have an opinion," she said. "We don't know anything about Cutler and what he's capable of."

"We know he's capable of murdering four people," Danny said. "Five if you count the van driver."

Hannah looked away. The truth was, she had wondered about Cutler, and though she felt terrible about wishing someone dead, she had to admit she would feel safer if he was permanently gone. Knowing she resembled Cutler's previous victims made her uneasy. She told herself she was being irrational. Cutler had seen her for less than a minute and then he had been focused on eluding capture. Finding her and hurting her would be the last thing on his mind.

But weren't serial killers psychopaths? They didn't operate according to normal rules of human behavior. Still, with everyone in three counties searching for him, it would be almost impossible for him to get anywhere near her, wouldn't it?

"Cut the chatter and let's call this meeting to order." Tony banged his coffee mug on the wooden bench at the front of the room. "Today, we're reviewing ground-search techniques and tactics."

Chairs creaked and papers rustled as everyone settled in to review the types of searches, the makeup of search teams, use of compass points and landmarks, gathering clues and other important details to remember. Before Hannah had joined Search and Rescue, she hadn't realized how science based some of their activities would be. Searchers had to be familiar not only with the topography of the area they were searching, but with how people tended to behave when lost, injured or trying to run away. Search and Rescue members had to be more than fit, willing volunteers. They had to devote hours to training and learning specialized skills and knowledge.

Halfway through a segment on planning a search, the headquarters phone rang at the same time Tony's cell phone vibrated. Immediately, tension radiated through the room. "Hello?" Tony answered the headquarters phone. He listened to the caller, making notes on the whiteboard mounted beside the phone. "We'll have a team right out," he said, and hung up.

"Car accident?" Danny was already on his feet.

"SUV rollover on Dixon Pass," Tony said. He scanned the room. "Hannah, I want you, Chris, Ryan and Ted. I'll coordinate from here in case we need life flight."

Hannah knew Danny wanted to protest. He was the type who wanted to go on every callout. But one look from Tony silenced him. Hannah pulled on her parka and followed the others to the next bay to retrieve the Beast.

The night was dark and clear, the cold cutting against her bare face as Hannah climbed into the back seat next to Ryan. Christine Mercer, a local artist with purple streaks in her short black hair, sat in the passenger seat next to Ted, who had insisted on driving. The oldest member of SAR, he fought hard to maintain the appearance of seniority. He was in terrific condition for a man who was sixty, but no one his age would have the stamina and strength of a twenty-something like Ryan, and Hannah sensed Ted was acutely aware of that.

SAR headquarters had been purposely located on the side of town nearest Dixon Pass and the ice climbing cliffs, two areas that accounted for at least half their emergency calls—maybe more than that in winter. The pass was the gateway to much of the backcountry terrain popular with skiers and climbers, and the road itself turned treacherous in inclement weather. Ten minutes after loading in, the Beast slowed as they approached flashing lights just this side of the top of Dixon Pass. The red-and-blue revolving lights cast kaleidoscope patterns across the black pavement and the snowy cliffs alongside.

"I bet the vehicle slid on ice," Ted said as he pulled the Beast in behind a highway patrol black-and-white. "It looks slick out here."

As Hannah exited the vehicle, she had a disorienting flash of déjà vu. The place she was standing was directly across the road from the spot where she had first seen Charlie Cutler.

"Come on," Chris said. She handed Hannah her gear bag and together they joined the group of law enforcement personnel and civilians by the side of the road. The four men and one woman were standing uphill from a black SUV that lay on its back like an upturned bug, one side resting against the rock cut that had been made when the road was built. The windshield was smashed and various bits of trim dangled from the vehicle, but it was in better shape than Hannah would have expected from a rollover.

"What's the situation?" Chris asked the highway patrolman closest to her.

"Looks like the driver got too close to the side, one or two wheels dropped off the edge of the pavement, he overcorrected and the vehicle rolled, then skidded to a stop against the wall here." The officer gestured.

"He's lucky he didn't roll the other way and the wall stopped him." At the sound of the familiar voice, Hannah looked past the highway patrolman to Deputy Jake Gwynn. He nodded in greeting, then gestured to the man and woman who sat on the ground by his patrol SUV. "We thought there was someone trapped in the vehicle but turns out we were wrong. The driver and passenger were able to get out of the vehicle on their own just before you arrived , but you might check them out."

"Nobody else in the car?" Ted asked.

"No one," the highway patrolman said. "Sorry about the false alarm."

Hannah introduced herself to the couple by

the sheriff's department vehicle. Both of them bore traces of white dust from their SUV's airbags. "How are you feeling?" she asked. "Any injuries? Cuts? Bruises? Any swelling? Anything hurt to move?"

"Maybe a few bruises," the man said.

"Mostly we're just shook up," the woman said. She looked across the road, where the pavement dropped off into the canyon. "When I think what could have happened if we'd been on the other side I feel sick."

"Let me check your vitals, make sure everything is okay," Hannah said.

They didn't protest as she looked them over. As they had said, the only consequences of their accident were a few bumps and bruises and a fright that would probably stay with them for a while. "Do you have someone you can call to come get you?" she asked when she was through.

"My brother is on his way from Junction," the man said. He looked at the upside-down SUV. "Do you think the insurance company will total it? I've only had it a few months."

"I'm sure it will work out," Hannah said as she repacked her gear. She wasn't even sure the man had been speaking to her, but it seemed the polite thing to say.

She left the couple and returned to the group

by the road. The other three members of the SAR team were ranged around the upside-down SUV, discussing the damage or the accident itself or maybe even what might have happened if the vehicle had been less sturdy or the driver and his passenger less lucky.

Jake was deep in conversation with the highway patrolman. As Hannah approached them, she overheard part of their conversation. "You should definitely get another year or so of local experience under your belt before you apply," the other officer was saying. "By then there should be a few more positions opening up."

"I figure the variety of investigations and situations I'll get with the sheriff's department will look good on my CV," Jake said. He glanced up and saw Hannah and smiled. "Everything okay with the driver and passenger?"

"They're going to be sore tomorrow, and they're still pretty shook up, but they should be okay." She set down the heavy gear bag. "He said his brother is on the way."

"Right. And a wrecker." Jake looked back at the vehicle. "At least we don't have to haul this one out of the valley."

"Were you in on that van that went over the side a few days ago?" the highway patrolman asked. "The one with Charlie Cutler?"

"Hannah was first on the scene," Jake said. "I came along just after her."

The patrolman turned to her. "I'm Phil Landers," he said. "It sounds like that whole situation was pretty hairy."

Hannah shrugged. The very nature of the work they did was "hairy," but she didn't feel like pointing that out. Today was an exception—they had showed up prepared to do everything from pulling someone out of the icy river below after climbing down to them across ice, rock and snow, to using the Jaws of Life to extract victims with multiple traumatic injuries, then establishing a place for the medical transport helicopter to land. Instead, everyone got to go home unharmed. It didn't happen like that very often.

"Here's the wrecker." Officer Landers nodded at the approaching vehicle. "I'd better get him lined out."

Jake moved closer to Hannah. "It's good to see you again," he said. "How are you?"

"I'm okay." She could pretend she hadn't heard his conversation with Landers, and spend the rest of her spare time wondering what it meant. Or she could risk offending him and ask. She didn't like uncertainty, so she opted to ask. "I caught some of what you were saying just now. Are you looking for a new job?"

"I like my job here," he said. "But eventually I'll probably want to move on, to somewhere with more opportunity for growth. A state job could provide that."

"I guess so." Logically, it made sense, though the idea that he could already be thinking of leaving when he had just got here didn't set well with her.

"No news on Cutler," he said—because he thought she wanted to know, or because he wanted to change the subject...or both?

"I heard a report on the radio this evening," she said. "Some of the rest of the crew were saying they think he's dead."

"It's a possibility," Jake agreed. "Not many people would survive for long in the wilderness in the middle of winter."

She met his eyes, and saw her own conviction reflected back at her. "You don't think he's dead, do you?" she asked.

"I don't." He moved closer still, his voice low. She could see the five-o'clock shadow along his jaw, and caught the scent of woodsmoke on his clothes. Did he have dinner at the barbecue place in town? "I've been reading the file Bernalillo County sent over," he said. "One thing I got from it is that Cutler is a planner. Cutler knew he was going to be transported. I don't think he merely seized the opportunity of the crash to get away. I think he caused the crash and had a plan. He knew where he wanted to go and what he wanted to do."

"Was he familiar with this area?" she asked.

"He wasn't from here, but it's possible he visited at one time. And you can learn a lot from internet research."

She wrapped her arms around herself, warding off a sudden chill. "You're not making me feel any better," she said.

"I promise if we hear anything about him, you'll be one of the first to know."

Why? she wanted to ask, but this time she didn't. There was a small bit of comfort in thinking that Cutler might be dead, or at least very far away from here.

Chapter Seven

After he admitted his ambition wasn't to stay with the Rayford County Sheriff's Department forever, Jake didn't miss the chill in Hannah's attitude that had nothing to do with the weather. He wanted to protest that he wasn't doing anything different from what a lot of other people did. Small departments like this were the perfect place for an officer to gain experience and learn on the job, but Rayford County would never have specialized divisions like vice or violent crime, or even its own SWAT team. With Rayford County, Jake could get a taste for investigation and forensics, but if he wanted to focus on those areas, he would need to look further afield. There wasn't anything wrong with that.

He was about to tell her as much when the rest of the Search and Rescue crew decided it was time to leave. Hannah said goodbye and turned away. Maybe he'd find the opportunity to talk to her later. He hoped so. He really liked her and wanted to get to know her better. After all, he planned to stay in Eagle Mountain a couple more years, at least, and after that he might very well land a job with highway patrol or even the Colorado Bureau of Investigations that would keep him in the area.

He was still brooding over this the next morning at the sheriff's department. Travis stopped by his desk. "How are you with dogs?" the sheriff asked.

"Dogs?" Jake sat up straighter. "Sir?"

"Yeah. Do you get along with them?"

"Yes, sir. I like dogs." There had always been multiple dogs on the ranch when he was growing up, mostly heelers and the occasional Australian shepherd. Their job was to help manage the livestock, but they all became family pets. One heeler, Lacy, had slept at the foot of Jake's bed for years.

"There's a stray who's been hanging around downtown," Travis said. "Nobody claims him. A couple of people have tried to catch him but they haven't had any luck. I need you to round him up and take him to the shelter in Junction."

"Wouldn't that be a job for, well, a dog catcher?" Jake asked.

"Today, that's you." Travis tapped the corner of the desk. "Last report, he was spotted in the alley behind the brewery. The kitchen help have probably been leaving scraps for him."

"Do you have a description?" Jake asked.

"Medium sized, brown, long legs, long ears, some kind of hound."

This was small-town law enforcement in a nutshell, Jake thought as he headed out on foot toward the brewery. One day you're tracking a dangerous killer; the next you're on the hunt for a stray hound.

At least it wasn't a bull that had jumped the fence. At his initial interview with the sheriff, Travis had told him his background in ranching was a mark in his favor. "We do a fair amount of putting back cattle that have gotten out of their pastures," Travis said. "They're valuable property for the ranchers, plus they're a traffic hazard if they wander around loose."

On his way out the door the office manager, Adelaide, waylaid him. "You'll need this," she said, and held out a purple leash.

"Thanks," he said, and tucked the leash in his pocket.

"Good luck," she said. "From what I hear, this pup is pretty skittish."

He walked a couple of blocks, then turned into the alley behind the brewery and slowed his steps, scanning the area for any sign of a brown hound. Snuffling noises led him to the dumpster, a long tail poking out from behind it. Leash in hand, he moved closer. "Come here, pup," he said softly.

The dog looked up, then charged past him. Jake stumbled back and almost fell. "Oh no, you don't!" he shouted, and the chase was on. He raced down the alley after the canine, and emerged onto the sidewalk, almost colliding with a large woman laden with packages.

"I'm sorry, ma'am," Jake said, stopping to retrieve a fallen parcel and return it to her.

"Was that your dog?" the woman asked, eyeing the leash in his hand.

"No, ma'am. Just a stray that I'm trying to catch."

"Well, watch where you're going."

"Yes, ma'am." Jake looked past her, searching for the dog. He caught a flash of brown fur across the street, in the vacant lot between an art gallery and a T-shirt shop, and crossed the street at a fast walk, leash in hand.

For the next hour, Jake pursued the dog over four blocks of downtown Eagle Mountain. Several times he got close enough to touch the tips of the dog's fur, but every time the dog darted away. He had obviously been on his own a while—he had the dirty, hungry look of neglect. He was definitely more frightened than fierce, and Jake was more determined than ever to get him to safety.

In the alley behind Mo's Tavern, Jake managed to grab hold of the dog's ruff. "It's okay, boy, I'm not going to hurt you," he murmured, and reached for the leash, now looped in his belt.

The dog lunged forward suddenly, sending Jake sprawling in the dirt of the alley.

"You're never going to catch him that way."

He looked up to see a young woman standing just outside the door to the tavern, a cigarette in one hand. Jake stood and brushed off his uniform. "I'm open to suggestions," he said.

"He's hungry. Try bribing him. Wait a minute." She stubbed out the cigarette in the bucket of sand by the door and disappeared into Mo's. A few seconds later she emerged with a paper to-go bag and handed it to Jake. "Boneless chicken wings. No sauce. It's his favorite."

"If you've been feeding him, why haven't you caught him?"

She smirked. "He's not hurting anyone."

"He looks in pretty rough shape to me," Jake said.

"He's better off running free than locked up in some shelter." She shrugged. "Give him the chicken. At least he'll have a meal."

Bag of chicken in hand, Jake continued to the end of the alley onto the street. "Hello, Deputy!"

Jake looked up to see Thad Richards striding toward him. "Good to see you again," Hannah's father said. "How are you doing?"

"Good." Jake looked past him. "Have you seen a brown dog around here?"

"A dog? What kind of dog?"

"Just…brown. Long ears. Kind of a hound?"

Thad joined Jake in scanning the street. "Can't say that I have. Has he done something wrong?"

"No, he's just a stray. I'm trying to catch him to take him to a shelter in Junction."

"Maybe you should just keep him. Dogs are really good company."

"That's not very practical," Jake said. "I live in an apartment."

"You have Becky Pratt's old place, above 1890 Antiques?"

Jake nodded. By now, he wasn't surprised that Thad knew this. There were very few secrets in a town this small.

"I know Becky," Thad said. "She loves animals. She won't mind you having a dog."

"I work pretty long hours. It wouldn't be fair to an animal to leave him alone so much."

"Take him to work with you. I mean, police

dogs do it. Maybe you could train him as a police dog."

Jake suppressed a laugh at the idea of that dog ever being police dog material. "Do you have a dog, Mr. Richards?" he asked. Maybe the hotel owner would like this one.

"We have three. Dachshunds. We love 'em. Hannah's crazy about dogs."

"I'm sure the shelter will find this dog a good home," Jake said. "But first, I have to catch him."

"Try liverwurst."

"Liverwurst?"

"My dogs go crazy for it. Smells to high heaven."

"I got some chicken from Mo's." He held up the grease-spotted paper bag.

Thad nodded. "That might work. But with the liverwurst, he'll be able to smell it from across town."

"Thanks for the tip. I'd better get back to work."

"Sure thing. Feel free to stop in at the Inn anytime. I think Hannah would like that."

This statement drew him up short. "Thanks. I'll do that."

"It's great having Hannah living with us, but I worry sometimes that she should be out on her own, not stuck here in this little town."

"Eagle Mountain is a good place to live," Jake said. "Hannah seems happy here, working as a paramedic and volunteering with Search and Rescue."

"Yes, but is she going to be happy doing that for the rest of her life? Maybe she should go to college, see more of the world." Thad shook his head. "You think about these things when you're a parent—wanting your kids to have opportunities you never had."

Why was Thad telling him all of this? And what was he supposed to say? "I'm sure Hannah will figure it out," he said. "Now I'd better see if I can find that dog."

"I'll tell Hannah you said hello."

Jake wasn't sure how Hannah would feel about that, but he didn't have much time to ponder the situation when the dog darted across the street right in front of him, a tall woman in pursuit. She drew up in front of Jake, panting. "That's the third time this week that dog has stolen food off the patio tables at the café," she said. "You've got to do something about him."

"I'm trying to catch him to take him to the shelter in Junction," Jake said.

The woman frowned. "You need to find his owners."

"I don't think he has an owner," Jake said.

The frown cut deeper lines into her face.

"People who would dump a dog deserve to be strung up by their thumbs," she said. She looked in the direction the dog had vanished. "I hope you catch him. I don't like the idea of him going hungry, but he can't steal food from my customers."

"Yes, ma'am. I'm on it."

Several times in the next hour, Jake thought of giving up, but if he went back to the station now he'd have to admit that a dog had outwitted him, and that stung his pride. Instead, he kept up a, well, dogged pursuit of the canine until, in late afternoon, he cornered him by yet another dumpster in yet another alley. But this alley had no outlet at the other end.

Jake stopped a few feet from the dog and squatted on the ground. "Hey there, pooch," he said in a gentle voice. "Are you as tired of running all over town as I am?"

The dog stood facing him, tongue out, panting. He had the typical hound dog's sad, brown eyes. Jake thought he was full grown, but not very old, and the outline of his ribs showed beneath his rough red-brown coat. Jake took out the chicken and unwrapped it. The dog's ears pricked up and he ran a big pink tongue across his lips.

There were three chicken wings. Three chances to earn the dog's trust and get close enough to slip the leash over his head and around his neck. Jack tossed one wing to him. It landed a few inches from his nose and the dog quickly gobbled it up.

"You've had a rough time of it, haven't you?" Jake asked. "You could probably use a friend." He tossed the second wing, and it landed halfway between him and the dog.

The dog hesitated, then took a few steps forward, grabbed up the wing, then retreated.

Jake held out the third wing. It was the largest of the three, gleaming with fat. The scent of it made Jake's mouth water—he could imagine what it must be doing to the dog.

The dog's nose twitched, and he licked his lips again. Then he gathered himself and lunged for the wing.

Jake was ready. He slipped the noose of the leash over the dog's head and pulled it tight. He didn't want to choke the animal, but he needed to be able to control him.

The dog's response surprised him. Instead of lunging and trying to get away, the dog looked up at him with a resigned expression, let out a sigh, and lay at his feet.

Jake tugged at the leash. "Come on," he said. "Come with me."

The dog rolled onto his side and lay there, panting.

Jake stared down at the animal. He tugged on the leash, but the dog's only response was a low moan.

"Come on," Jake pleaded. "I can't drag you."

Another moan from the dog, and a *thwap* of his tail against the packed dirt of the alley.

And that was how Jake ended up carrying forty pounds of hound dog through the streets of Eagle Mountain to the sheriff's department, to the amusement of many passersby, several of whom took out their cell phones to capture the scene. Jake ignored them, just as he tried to ignore the ripe odor of the dog in his arms, a smell that called to mind dirty floors, old shoes and something that had died some time ago.

The sheriff and Adelaide had both gone home for the day when Jake entered the sheriff's department. Deputy Shane Ellis looked up as Jake staggered in with the canine, then rose in alarm. "Is he hurt?" Shane asked. "Do we need to call the vet?"

"He's not hurt." Jake set the dog on the floor. The animal shook himself, then looked up, wagging his tail.

"What are you going to do with him?" Shane asked.

"I'm going to take him to the shelter in Junction."

Shane checked his watch. "I'm pretty sure

they're closed now. You'll have to wait until morning."

"Great." Jake stared down at the dog, who looked back up at him with hopeful eyes. "What am I supposed to do with him until then?"

"There's nobody in the cells," Shane said. "He should be safe in there."

The two of them, followed by the dog, walked downstairs to the basement holding cells. The dog followed them inside and Jake got a bowl of water for him and shut the door.

"He should be happy in there," Shane said.

They left the dog lapping up water, and headed back upstairs. As soon as they were out of sight, the howling began, a mournful, melodious bugling that could probably be heard on the next street over.

The two men exchanged looks. "That's going to draw some complaints," Shane said.

"I've got to stay around and finish up some paperwork," Jake said. "I'm sure he'll quiet down in a little bit."

Shane nodded. "I'm on patrol tonight," he said. "I'll head out."

He left, but the howling continued. For the next half hour, as Jake tried to focus on paperwork, the noise didn't cease or decrease in volume.

Finally, Jake returned to the cells. As soon as

the dog spotted him, he stopped howling and walked to the door of the cell, tail wagging.

"People are going to think I'm torturing you," Jake said. He knelt in front of the cell and scratched the dog's ears. The dog sank onto his haunches and moaned, eyes closed.

Jake checked the time. It was after six thirty. He was hungry and needed a shower. He couldn't stay here all night babysitting this dog. But he couldn't leave the dog here to disturb the peace, either. Finally he sighed and stood, and retrieved the leash. "Come on," he told the dog. "I guess you're coming home with me. But just for tonight."

ANOTHER WEEK SLIPPED by with no further sightings of Charlie Cutler. Hannah decided the people who said he had died out there in the wilderness were right. She put the whole episode out of her mind and focused on her work with the paramedics and at the hotel, and her volunteer job with Search and Rescue. All three activities kept her so busy she scarcely had time to sleep. A rash of house fires, home mishaps, heart attacks and traffic accidents kept the ambulance on the road most days, and mishaps among ice climbers and backcountry skiers led to a record number of Search and Rescue callouts for February.

The call to search for a missing skier late in the month found Hannah, Ted, Danny, SAR Lieutenant Carrie Andrews, Austen and Tony in a snowy basin high in the mountains, with a trio of friends who had become separated from a fourth companion during a cross-country trek between the ski huts.

"Mitch Anderson," a man in a yellow ski jacket and black helmet introduced himself. "I'm the one who called."

"Tell us what happened, Mr. Anderson," Tony said.

"Al—Al Grantham—was behind the rest of us, but not too far," Mitch said. "We lost sight of him and stopped at the top of a hill to wait for him. When he didn't show up after ten minutes, Del and I went back to look for him."

"We skied to the last place we'd all been together and tried to follow his tracks from there," a petite woman in a purple ski helmet said. "We thought we were following his tracks, but there are so many, going in all directions."

"We decided we'd better call for help before one of the rest of us got lost, or we got too far off the main trail and triggered an avalanche," Mitch said.

"You were smart to do that," Tony said. "Take us to the last place you saw him."

They skied single file along the ridgetop trail.

The day was clear and calm, the single-digit temperatures moderated by the intense sun and lack of wind. A beautiful day for a backcountry outing. Hannah hoped the group's memory of their beautiful day wasn't about to be ruined.

She estimated they had skied perhaps a quarter mile when they stopped. "We were all together here," Mitch said. "We stopped to take a picture. When the rest of us went on, Al said he'd be along in a minute."

"Why was he hanging back?" Tony asked.

"I thought he just, you know, needed to relieve himself or something. We'd been skiing a couple of hours since we left the last hut. But Al is a good, fast skier. I figured he'd catch up soon."

Tony studied the crisscrossing ski tracks across the top of the ridge. No tracks veered into the soft snow on either side. "Could he have turned around?" he asked. "Gone back for something?"

"I can't imagine why he'd do that," Mitch said.

"What is your friend wearing?" Tony asked.

"Orange ski pants, a blue jacket and a black helmet," the woman, Del, said. "He's a big guy, so he should be easy to spot."

"He had a red bandanna, too," Mitch said.

"From a Killington resort. He grew up in that area."

Tony nodded. "Hannah, you and Austen go back down the trail toward the second hut," he said. "Radio if you spot anything." He scanned the area. "I haven't had any reports of new avalanches in this area, but let's check our transceivers."

Hannah dutifully pulled out her avalanche transceiver, which had been on since they left the parking lot. Tony ran through the tests to make sure the devices were working in both transmit and search mode. If someone was buried in an avalanche—or even hurt and separated from the group—others could search for the signal and locate them.

"When you get to the hut, stay put and radio in for further instructions," Tony said. "The rest of us are going to check out some of these side paths." He indicated some faint trails that looked too old to have been made by the man they were looking for. But sun and wind could obscure fresh tracks or make old ones look newer, so they had learned to follow every avenue in a search.

Hannah led the way down the trail toward the hut, with Austen following. She hadn't worked with him much, though they had partnered once in a climbing exercise and he had proved himself competent and dependable. He was the newest member of the team and she didn't know him well. He had moved to Eagle Mountain from Denver and seemed eager to involve himself in his new community. "Have you done searches like this before?" he asked.

"A few. More in summer than winter, looking for missing hikers." She had been involved in some avalanche rescues, too, or rather, body searches, since they had never managed to find anyone alive. She shook off the grim memories.

"It's kind of eerie, isn't it?" He looked around them, at the expanse of snow. "It's so big, it makes me feel insignificant. And exposed."

Another shiver went through her. Now that Austen had mentioned it, she did feel exposed—vulnerable. In their bright ski clothes they were very visible against the white snow. Anyone with a pair of binoculars or even good vision would be able to track their progress along the ridge from a long way off.

She had had the same feeling the night she and Danny accompanied Jake and Gage to search for Charlie Cutler—the uneasiness of realizing what a target you presented for a killer with a gun. She tried to shrug off the sensation. "No one cares that we're here," she said.

"You're right." He gave a nervous laugh. "I need to remember that."

They continued along the trail. "What do you think happened?" Austen asked after a moment. "I mean to the guy we're looking for."

"Al." It always helped to think of the person by name. They weren't a vague statistic or a job to do, but a real person who needed help. Remembering that kept you going when you were cold or tired or wishing you were anywhere but out looking for them.

"Yeah. Why didn't Al catch up with his friends?" Austen said.

"Maybe Tony is right and he decided to ski back this way," she said. "Maybe he remembered that he left something at the ski hut."

"He should have let his friends know."

"He probably thought he could get there and back before they missed him. Or before they missed him enough to call for help. Maybe he thought he was closer to the hut than he was. Or he could have gotten disoriented and skied down one of the side trails." It was easy to get lost up here with few landmarks to guide you.

"That wasn't very smart," Austen said.

"Our whole job is necessary because people make not-so-smart decisions all the time," she said. "It's part of being human."

"Some of the people we help aren't doing anything dumb," he said. "They're just in the wrong place at the wrong time. The road ices over and they can't see the ice, or another car forces them to swerve the wrong way, or the ice they're climbing has a flaw they can't see and it gives way."

"It's not a good idea to try to fix blame on anyone," Hannah said. "We're about helping, not judging."

"I guess so," he said, though he didn't sound convinced.

Hannah picked up the pace, partly to reach their destination more quickly, and partly to put some distance between Austen and his questions. She didn't want to talk any more. She'd rather focus on the search, scanning the area around her for any sign of a disturbance.

They were within sight of the second hut when a flash of color in the snow ahead made Hannah wobble in midstride. Not orange or blue like the clothes of the man they were looking for, but red. A splash of red, like blood on the snow.

Or blood on the body of a man, stripped of all his clothing and lying in the snow twenty yards off the trail.

Chapter Eight

"How are you on cross-country skis?" Deputy Dwight Prentice stopped by Jake's desk a little after three o'clock and posed the question.

"I do all right," Jake said. Eastern Colorado had plenty of snow, but no mountains, so he had grown up cross-country skiing. "Why?"

"We just got a call from Search and Rescue," Dwight said. "They were called out to search for a skier who went missing between the first and second huts, above Delaware Basin. They found his body. Looks like murder."

Jake shoved back his chair and stood. "Maybe Charlie Cutler didn't die out there after all."

"Maybe not. Anyway, the easiest way to get up there is to ski the trail. Search and Rescue is waiting for us."

"I'll need to borrow some skis. I didn't bring mine with me." That was an oversight he would have to correct the next time he visited his parents.

A scuffling noise beneath Jake's desk distracted them. A brown dog, cleaner than before and already beginning to fill out, emerged, wagging his tail. "Why do you have a dog under your desk?" Dwight asked.

"He's the stray who was running loose around town." The dog shoved his head beneath Jake's hand and Jake rubbed the velvety ears. "He howls like crazy if I try to leave him alone."

Dwight smirked. "I thought you were supposed to take him to the shelter in Junction."

Jake looked down at the dog, who regarded him with worshipful eyes. "Yeah, well, by the time I caught him the shelter was closed. I took him home for the night and I guess I never quite made it out to the shelter."

Dwight laughed. "You sucker." He leaned over and patted the dog. "What's his name?"

"I'm calling him Gus. It seems to suit him."

"Does the sheriff know he's here?"

"Not exactly." Jake pulled on his jacket.

"He can't come to a crime scene with us," Dwight said. "Especially not up in the high country."

Jake frowned at the dog. If he left Gus at his apartment, his howling would be sure to draw complaints. He couldn't leave him to run loose at the sheriff's department. "I guess I'll have to figure something out."

"You'll need to find some skis, too. I think Mountain Outfitters will rent you some."

"I'll take care of it," Jake said, an idea forming. He might be able to solve the problem of the skis and the dog at the same time. "I'll take care of Gus, too."

"Make it quick," Dwight said. "Can you meet me back here in half an hour?"

"You bet."

Gus took his now-usual position in the back seat of the sheriff's department SUV. He had wanted to ride in the passenger seat, but the image of himself with the dog as his partner had been a little too cutesy for Jake to bear, so he had insisted the dog ride in back, shielded from public view by the heavily tinted back windows.

Jake found a parking spot directly in front of the Alpiner Inn, snapped the leash on Gus's collar and led the dog inside.

"Well, hello there!" Thad Richards greeted them from behind the front counter when they entered. "I see you have a friend there, Deputy."

"This is Gus," Jake said. "I was wondering if you could watch him for a few hours while I'm on a call."

"Sure, we could do that." Thad came out from behind the counter and squatted down to greet the dog.

"I have another favor to ask, too," Jake said.

"I need to borrow some cross-country gear—skis and boots, and those insulated coveralls you loaned me before. I promise I'll get my own gear soon."

"No problem." Thad stood. "I'll get them right now."

He disappeared into the back of the hotel and a few moments later, Brit Richards emerged. "Hello, Deputy," she said. "Thad told me we're going to be dog sitting." She smiled at Gus, who wiggled his entire rear end in greeting.

"I hope you don't mind," Jake said. He unclipped the leash and Gus hurtled forward and stood with his front paws on the counter. "Down!" Jake commanded.

"It's all right. He won't hurt anything." Brit rubbed his ears. "Aren't you a pretty boy?" She looked at Jake. "Where did you get him?"

"He was a stray," Jake said, not wanting to go into the whole story. "He doesn't like being alone."

Thad emerged from the back room, loaded down with skis, boots and coveralls. Jake hurried forward to relieve him of the burden. "Thanks so much," he said.

"Is something wrong?" Brit looked worried. "Does this have anything to do with the call Hannah went on a little earlier?"

"Maybe." Jake balanced the borrowed skis

and clothing. "As far as I know, all the Search and Rescue personnel are fine. Sorry I can't stay to talk—I need to get on the road. Thanks for looking after Gus."

He hurried out the door and into his SUV. He'd have to buy the Richardses a gift card for the nicest place in town to thank them for being such a big help.

Twenty minutes later, he and Dwight were strapping on skis. They headed up the trail toward Hut #2, and within thirty minutes he spotted the peaked roof of the hut, and just beyond that, the cluster of people gathered at the side of the trail.

He searched for Hannah and found her, standing to one side, her arms hugged across her chest as she spoke with the SAR commander, Tony. "Someone's covered the body," Dwight said. "They shouldn't have done that."

Sure enough, the body was hidden beneath a silver emergency blanket. Tony looked up and spotted them and joined them as they kicked off their skis. "Before you say anything, I promise we didn't touch the body or disturb it in any way," he said. "But we had to cover it. His friends were freaking out about the state of him."

"What is the state of him?" Dwight asked.

"Naked. And it looks like his throat has been cut. There's a lot of blood."

Dwight nodded. "I can see how that would be upsetting."

Hannah and another man moved in behind Tony. "We found him," Hannah said.

The man with her nodded. "He was just lying out there in the open, blood everywhere." He swallowed hard. "It was pretty shocking."

"What's your name?" Jake asked.

"Austen. Austen Morrissey."

"We'll get your statement in a minute, Mr. Morrissey," Jake said. He moved over beside Hannah. "You okay?" he asked, keeping his voice low.

She nodded. "It was a shock."

"How long had he been missing when you found him?" Jake asked.

"Close to two hours. His friends waited an hour before they called us out."

He nodded. "Stick around. I'll probably have more questions after we've looked at him."

Dwight was already kneeling beside the covered body when Jake joined him. "The snow around here is really disturbed," Dwight said. "Some of it is probably from the SAR team but those tracks might be the killer's." He indicated a set of ski tracks setting out from the body. "Better radio for backup."

While Jake put in the call, Dwight carefully lifted the emergency blanket from the body. The man beneath it was tall—Jake guessed over six feet—and fit, with sandy hair and beard, a tattoo of snakes and flowers down his left arm, the ink standing out against his pale, pale skin. Blood stained his chest and bloomed on the snow around him from the gash in his neck. "Deputy Green's throat was cut, too," Jake said. "It's how Cutler killed all his victims."

"His murderer took his skis, helmet, gloves, goggles and every stitch of clothing," Dwight said. "That points to Cutler, too. He would have wanted all those things."

"How did he get close enough to cut his throat?" Jake looked around them. "You can't sneak up on anyone out here."

"Maybe he pretended to need help," Dwight said. "Most people wouldn't ignore someone stranded or hurt up here, so far from other aid." He straightened. "Let's talk to his friends, then to the SAR volunteers."

The victim's three friends huddled together out of sight of the man's body, arms around each other. The woman had been crying, while the two men looked grim. Dwight and Jake introduced themselves, then listened to their story of an outing among friends gone wrong. "I don't know why he would have turned back," the woman, Del, said.

"You say you had lunch at the ski hut," Dwight said. "Could he have left something behind there and gone to retrieve it?"

"I can't imagine what," she said.

"We weren't even there that long," one of the men said. "And if he did go back, why didn't he tell us?"

"Did you see anyone else while you were out here this morning?" Jake asked. "Someone in the distance, or anyone near the hut?"

All three shook their heads. "There's never many people up here during the week," Del said.

Jake nodded. He and Dwight had seen no one else on the way up here.

"Was he the type of person to go out of his way to help someone else?" Jake asked.

"Yes." Del didn't hesitate to answer. "He would stop on the side of the road to change a stranger's tire, and he always gave money to street people." She sniffed. "I can't believe someone would do this to him."

One of the men put his arm around her and looked at the two deputies. "Do you think this has anything to do with that man who went missing up here a while back? I read he was a convicted murderer."

"We don't know," Dwight said.

"We saw the posters about him at the trailhead," the other man said. "But we didn't pay much attention. Maybe we should have."

And maybe the sheriff's department should have insisted on closing the area to all recreation, though local officials had balked at the idea, Jake thought. And with no sign of Cutler for almost two weeks, closures would have been difficult to enforce. He and Dwight took the contact information of the three and told them they were free to go, then moved over to the SAR team.

Hannah and the rest of her team were gathered to the side of the trail, sipping coffee from thermoses. Dwight and Jake split them up to interview them. The group that had taken the side trail reported they had seen nothing unusual. "I don't think the trail had been used much since the last fresh snow," Carrie, a sturdy thirty-something blonde, said. "We turned around as soon as Hannah radioed that she and Austen had found the body."

"Did you see anyone at all while you were up here, other than the dead man's friends?" Dwight asked.

"No one," Tony said.

No one else had anything useful to add. By the time they had collected everyone's statements, Sergeant Gage Walker and Deputy Ronin

Doyle had arrived to help process the scene. The SAR team headed back down the mountain and the sheriff's department personnel set to work. "I want to follow those tracks and see where they lead," Jake said, indicating the ski tracks leading away from Al Grantham's body.

"Good idea," Gage said. "But be careful. If this is Cutler, he's still armed and we know he won't hesitate to kill a cop."

"Right," Jake said. Nothing like setting out across a wide-open expanse of terrain, feeling as if you had a target on your back.

Dwight and Jake set out, skiing parallel on either side of the tracks, alternately scanning the area around them, and watching the ground for any evidence the skier might have dropped. "If this is Cutler, where has he been for the past two weeks?" Dwight asked.

"There must be summer cabins up here he could break into and stay for a while," Jake said. "He was injured in the car wreck when he escaped. Maybe he was healing before he set out again."

"You know some people are going to say we stopped looking for him too soon," Dwight said.

"We threw everything we had into searching for him for three days after he escaped," Jake said. "We didn't have the resources to keep it up." But it was hard to believe they couldn't have done more. A man was dead, and they might have been able to prevent it. The thought galled.

After about fifteen minutes, Jake stopped. "What is it?" Dwight asked.

"He's skiing parallel to the trail," he said. He indicated the ridge above them. "He's far enough away, and far enough down in elevation that someone on the trail would be unlikely to see him unless they were looking."

"Are you sure they couldn't see him?" Dwight looked up toward the trail. "I think I could see someone on the trail."

"You might be able to see the top of their head," Jake said. "Or more likely, hear their voice. But look how the terrain undulates. The snow has drifted. I don't think someone up there would notice him unless they looked very carefully."

"Where's he going?" Dwight asked. "The trail leads to the first hut."

"Maybe he went there."

But well before they reached the first hut, the tracks turned upward, crossed the ridge and the main trail, and set off on a parallel course on the opposite side of the trail. The terrain was much rougher here, less open. "It would be easier for him to hide here," Jake said, as they picked their way around a trio of snow-covered boulders.

"You can't see the trail at all from here," Dwight said.

"No, but you'd be able to hear anyone talking. Sound carries. Listen." They stopped and the murmur of conversation from somewhere above drifted down. Jake couldn't make out any words, but he could track the movement of people on the trail by the sounds of their voices.

"What's he doing, going back the way he came?" Dwight asked. "Is he tracking the rest of Al's party? Planning to kill them also?"

"I don't know," Jake said. "He killed Al to steal his skis and clothing. I don't know if he'd risk attacking a group of three. Maybe he wanted to see what they would do—if they would go back and find the body."

"Or maybe he wanted to see who else showed up," Dwight said. "Like law enforcement."

"Or Search and Rescue," Jake said. He stopped again, the thought hitting him like a blow to the chest.

"What is it?" Dwight asked. "What's wrong?"

Jake shook his head. "It may be nothing."

"What? What did you think of?"

He met his fellow deputy's gaze. "Hannah is the only member of Search and Rescue who saw Cutler the day he escaped from custody. And he got a good look at her. She looks like the women he killed—and the other women he's suspected of killing."

"You think he was tracking her," Dwight said.

"I hope I'm wrong," Jake said. But the knot in his gut told him this hunch was too big to ignore. If Cutler had fixated on Hannah—if he had remained in the area because of her, even—then he was going to be a bigger problem than they had anticipated.

"CHARLIE CUTLER CAN'T be after me," Hannah protested when Jake told her about the ski tracks and his theory. The rest of the SAR team had already started back toward the parking area, but Jake had asked her to stay to talk with him. "He doesn't even know me. He saw me once, for all of fifteen seconds."

"If I'm right and he was trailing the SAR team, he saw you for longer than that." Jake shoved his hands into his pockets and began to pace, his skis still stuck in the snow beside the trail. "I read his psychological profile in the file Bernalillo County sent over," he said. "He has a pattern of choosing a victim—usually after a chance encounter—and stalking her. One of the women he killed was a barista in a coffee shop he visited once. Another was a passenger on a bus he rode. The profiler said he has a type and feels compelled to follow and kill them."

The idea that a known murderer could be stalking her was terrifying—and surreal. She looked around at the sunlit snowscape. What had been beautiful before now seemed menacing. "Where is he now?" she asked. "Where did the tracks lead?"

"They stopped at the edge of a ravine." He shrugged. "They just…stopped."

"Did he go down in the ravine? Did he fall?"

Jake shook his head. "We don't know. The tracks went right up to the edge, then there wasn't any sign of him. No footprints. No disturbed rocks—nothing."

"He didn't just vanish."

"We've called for a tracking dog and more searchers. Maybe he backtracked and we didn't see it. Or maybe he did something to hide his tracks. We'll figure it out."

She wished she shared his conviction. If Charlie Cutler had managed to survive up here on his own for the past two weeks, what was to keep him from eluding them indefinitely? "What am I supposed to do in the meantime?" she asked. "I can't quit my job and hide in my room."

"Maybe you could take a leave of absence or…"

"No. That isn't possible or practical. We don't even know if this man is a real threat to me."

"I'm not willing to take a chance that he is."

"Then find him."

He looked pained. "We're going to. But in the meantime, you could be in real danger."

She struggled to rein in her frustration. "I appreciate your concern, and I promise I'll be careful. But I can't stop my life—or let down the people who are depending on me—because of a threat that might not even be real."

He pressed his mouth into a thin line, and she was sure he was going to argue with her, but he only shook his head and moved toward his skis. "I'll go with you to your car."

"Thank you." She wasn't foolish enough to suggest striking out on her own when Charlie Cutler might be nearby.

They set out skiing. He let her take the lead and she soon fell into a familiar rhythm, gliding along the trail, enjoying the exertion and the warm sun on her face. She wasn't going to think about the dead man, or the live one who might or might not be stalking her, or anything but this moment.

That was the theory, anyway. Getting her mind to stick to that plan was another. For now, she was grateful for the man with the gun who skied right behind her. Though why she had faith Jake could do anything against a man who seemed to appear and disappear at will, she couldn't say. Maybe she was merely comforted by the idea that she wasn't entirely alone in this.

Her Subaru sat apart from the half-dozen law enforcement vehicles that now filled the parking lot, including two new arrivals, one of which included a German shepherd with a coat that proclaimed Canine Officer. She noted the vehicle was from neighboring Delta County.

She turned to Jake. "Thank you for seeing me back to my car," she said. "I'll be okay now."

"I'll wait until you're inside the car," he said. "With the door locked."

She refrained from rolling her eyes, and carried her skis to the car. She loaded them into the rack atop the car, aware of him watching, then circled around to the driver's side and started to climb in. Halfway in, she froze.

"What's wrong?" Jake hurried to her side.

She pointed to the windshield. A scrap of red cloth fluttered from beneath the wiper blade. "That wasn't there when I left," she said.

Carefully, Jake lifted the wiper blade and caught the edge of the cloth with a gloved thumb and forefinger. "It's part of a bandanna," he said. He held it up and she stared at the words Ski Killington in white script across one corner. "Al Grantham was wearing a Killington bandanna," she said, her voice pinched and strained sounding.

Charlie Cutler had taken that bandanna. He had left it here as a message. One that said, *I know you. I'm watching you.*

Chapter Nine

The enormity of finding one man in this vast area struck Jake as a law enforcement team gathered at the trailhead nearest the second hut to conduct a ground search. Not a single structure or even a tree broke the expanse of snow and sky that spread out in every direction. Even with sunglasses the glare of the sun off the snow made him squint, and once they began to move out across the landscape he lost all sense of direction.

They were searching for any clues Charlie Cutler might have left behind, but what those clues might be no one could say. A forensics team had combed the area around Al Grantham's body and both of the closest ski huts, but as far as Jake knew, they had come up with nothing. Gage had bagged the bandanna left on Hannah's car and dusted the car itself for fingerprints, but the windshield and every part of the car Cutler might even have brushed against had been wiped clean. They had questioned the few people who had been in the parking lot, but no one had seen anyone suspicious, or anyone near Hannah's car.

Then again, Cutler wouldn't have looked suspicious. He would have looked like anyone else in the area at that time—a man with skis, wearing a helmet, goggles and bulky ski clothes that would have made him unrecognizable to almost anyone, even those who might know him well, which no one here did.

Jake wanted to find Cutler, to see that he was punished for his crimes, to prevent him from harming other people, but most of all to protect Hannah. He had felt her terror when she had spotted the bandanna on her car and realized who must have put it there.

But wanting something very badly wasn't enough. It was going to take more than will to find Cutler in these rugged mountains. Ski tracks crisscrossed the area nearest the parking lot. The tracks grew fewer as they moved farther from the road, but wind picked up the snow and sent it swirling across the ground to settle once more yards away, leaving the surface as smooth and even as if swept by a broom. He moved steadily forward, scanning the ground with little hope of finding anything. Ten feet on either side of him, other law enforcement officers did the same, but even that bit of order disintegrated quickly as deep gorges or icy cliffs forced them to deviate from straight lines.

Occasionally, he heard the throb of helicopter blades from the air search, but the vastness of the landscape swallowed up even that sound before the chopper was out of sight. The crunch of his skis on hard-packed snow and the whistle of the wind against his helmet was the primary soundtrack for the search.

By three o'clock the peaks to the west sent long shadows over the landscape. A deeper chill set in, and Jake found he was exhausted, even though he felt he hadn't done anything. His head throbbed dully—probably from not drinking enough water. He forced himself to drain the water reservoir in his pack as he joined the others in the parking lot. "The air search didn't spot anything, either," Gage reported.

"Will they try again tomorrow?" someone behind Jake asked.

"Not unless we have another sighting that helps us narrow our focus," Gage said.

Another sighting or another murder, Jake thought grimly. But what else could they do? There was too much territory to cover. Too many places for a man like Cutler, who had been trained in stealth, to disappear.

"YOUR BLOOD PRESSURE is one-twenty over eighty-three, Gail. Right where it was last time."

Hannah slipped the stethoscope from her ears and unfastened the blood pressure cuff.

Gail Hunnicutt, a regular on the hike-and-bike trail that ran past the fire station, stood and pulled on her coat. "Thanks for checking for me, Hannah. I'll go home and write it down on the sheet I keep for my doctor."

"Anytime. Have a good rest of the day." She waved goodbye to the older woman and was surprised to see Danny slip in as Gail exited.

The sight of Danny was jarring. She had expected to see Jake, since he made it a point of stopping by every day to check on her. She couldn't decide if it was endearing or annoying—probably a little of both.

"Hey," Danny said.

"Hey, yourself." She stowed the blood pressure cuff in a drawer and replaced the stethoscope on its hook and faced him. "What are you doing here?" Danny hadn't shown up at the fire station since the two of them had split up.

"It's almost quitting time for you, isn't it?" He leaned against the wall beside the door, arms crossed over his chest. "I thought I'd see if you wanted to grab a beer."

"Danny." She drew out his name. What was he playing at?

"Just friends." He smiled, and she tried to ignore the tug in her chest, left over from the early days when she had been so besotted with him—before she figured out that the two of them together were never going to work long-term.

"I thought maybe you'd want to relax a little," he said. "You've had kind of a rough week."

Understatement. Charlie Cutler—what he had done, where he might be, where he would strike next—was all anyone wanted to talk about. Most people didn't know about the "message" he had left under the wiper blade of her car, but everyone knew about the murder of Al Grantham, and they all speculated on how Cutler had survived in the snowy wilderness so long. Add in a week of callouts for her regular job and two SAR expeditions—one for a fallen ice climber, another for a person trapped in a car by a snowslide—and she was wrung out. Suddenly sitting in a cozy tavern and having a beer sounded like exactly what she needed. Especially since her only other alternative was going home to the inn and having her mom and dad fret over her.

"Sure," she said. "Are you buying?"

He grinned. "The first round, anyway."

Twenty minutes later, they had walked across the park to Mo's, and settled at a high table across from the bar. "Any more news on Charlie Cutler?" Danny asked as a server set two mugs of draft in front of them.

"No. And talking about him isn't my idea of relaxing."

"Sorry, I just figured you'd be the first to know, since you're so tight with that deputy."

"Do you mean Jake? We aren't tight." They weren't anything. Not really. He had decided she could be Cutler's next victim, so he kept checking on her. And yeah, he'd stopped by the inn a few times with his new dog, but that was mostly to talk fishing or skiing with her dad. He was just a friendly guy who was passing through on his way to some place bigger and better.

"I see you with him all the time," Danny said.

"What, are you spying on me?"

He laughed. "Hard to miss the cop car parked in front of the inn all the time, or over at the fire station."

"There's nothing between me and Deputy Gwynn." She took a sip of beer, then set down her glass and fixed him with a hard look. "But even if there were, it's none of your business."

"Hey, I'm still your friend. I care what happens to you. I'd hate to see you hurt."

"What make you think Jake would hurt me?"

"You told me the reason you and I couldn't be a couple was because you're looking for a long-term commitment and I'm not," he said. "And you're right about me. But Deputy Jake isn't your long-term man, either. He's got short-timer written all over him. He's here to get some experience for his résumé and move on. It's practically built into the job."

"Not everyone who hires on with the sheriff's department leaves," she said. For every deputy who moved on, there were others who were making a career with the department.

"The people who stay are from here," Danny said. "Or they came here looking for something specific this place has to offer. Jake doesn't fall into either of those categories."

"You're probably right." She shrugged. "And it doesn't matter, because Jake and I aren't involved."

"So you're not dating anyone right now," he said.

"No." She drank more beer, mainly so she wouldn't be tempted to elaborate—to tell him she was "taking a break" or some other excuse. Only two months had passed since they'd agreed to call it quits and she didn't have to explain herself to him.

He leaned toward her across the table and spoke in a quieter voice. "In that case, what do you think about taking our friendship in a different direction?"

"What are you talking about?"

"We'd still be friends," he said. "But friends with benefits. And hey—" He held up a hand to silence her protest. "Before you work yourself up over the idea, think a minute—we were good together. You can't deny that. We had a lot of fun. And I really miss you. Maybe you miss me, too."

She stared at him, torn between telling him off and agreeing to what she knew would be a stupid idea. Because Danny was right—the two of them had been good together. Deciding to break if off with him hadn't been easy. But it had been the right decision. "I guess since you can't have me anymore, now I'm irresistible," she said, trying to inject the words with sarcasm.

"Hey, I never stopped wanting you, babe." He reached for her hand, but she pulled it away and pushed back her chair.

"No, thanks," she said. "I don't think I'd be good at an arrangement like that."

"You never know until you try." He grinned—the same boyish, goofy grin that had won her over so many times before. But not tonight.

"Thanks for the beer," she said, and left.

The cold night air hit her like a slap, clearing her head a little. She stopped to zip up her parka and pull on gloves, then set off across the park, old snow crunching beneath her boots. She was halfway across the playground area when someone called her name.

She turned to see Jake being pulled toward her by a large brown hound. "Hello, Gus," she said, rubbing the dog's ears. "And hello, Jake."

"Hello." He looked down at the dog. "Gus, sit."

The dog stared up at him, wagging his tail.

Jake reached into his pocket and took out a treat. "Sit," he repeated.

Gus sat with a thump! He snatched the treat as soon as it was within range, then immediately popped back up. "He's a work in progress," Jake said.

"Is he still going to work with you?" she asked.

"Yes. When I'm in the office he hangs out under my desk, and he rides in the back seat of the cruiser. I keep waiting for someone to object, but so far, no one has."

"He's obviously bonded with you." She rubbed the dog's chin and he leaned toward her hand, in danger of falling over.

"What are you doing out here by yourself?" he asked.

"Just walking back to my car from Mo's. And before you say anything, I didn't even have half a beer."

"I wasn't going to say anything." He studied her more closely. "Are you okay? You look a little upset."

"It's nothing." She wasn't about to share her conversation with Danny. She'd like to pretend it had never happened.

"Are you sure? You haven't seen anything suspicious, or that made you feel unsafe? It doesn't matter if you think it isn't important. You can tell me."

His genuine concern touched her. "Really, it's nothing like that," she said. "Just a stupid argument with someone I know. Nothing important."

"Good." But he didn't relax. "I'll walk you to your car," he said, and fell into step beside her. She noticed he wasn't in uniform, but wore gray knit joggers and tennis shoes, and a worn leather jacket with a black lamb's-wool collar.

"So what have you been up to?" she asked.

He shrugged. "Just the usual. I returned a lost wallet to a tourist and took a report from a store manager about a shoplifter who has since vanished."

"So…no news about Charlie Cutler?"

He didn't answer right away, and she began to feel uneasy. "*Is* there news about Cutler?" she asked.

"I wasn't going to say anything. I didn't want to upset you."

She wrapped her arms around herself. "Too late for that. What is it? Has something happened?"

"A man who owns a cabin in the high country snowmobiled up there to check on things and found someone had broken in. It was Cutler."

"How can you be so sure?"

"There were fingerprints. A perfect match for Cutler."

"That was a lucky break," she said.

"No luck involved," he said. "He went to a lot of trouble to leave very clear prints on a glass where we would see them. He wanted us to know he was there."

"Why would he do that?"

"I'm not qualified to answer that, but I don't like that he's still in the area. Why is he staying around here?"

Unless he's waiting to kill me, she thought, but she couldn't say the words out loud. Speaking them would make the threat too real. "I haven't seen or heard anything at all threatening or unusual," she said. "And I've been hypervigilant."

He nodded. "That's all we can do. We're combing the area up there, searching for him. And we're plastering every trailhead and cabin with posters warning people to stay away, and to report any sign of him to us."

They reached her car and she fished out her keys. "Thanks for letting me know," she said. "And thanks for walking me to my car."

"Where are you headed now?" he asked.

"Home, I guess."

"Want to get something to eat?"

Was he asking her out? "Where?"

He looked down at the dog. "My place? It's easier than leaving him in the car while we go in. I'm not a bad cook."

The idea appealed to her. Eating at his place was private, unlikely to attract the attention of gossips. And it wasn't the inn, where her parents tried to pretend they weren't worried and only magnified her own anxiety. "Thanks," she said. "I'd like that." If nothing else, she could use the evening to find out more about Jake's plans for the future. How long did he see himself staying in the area—and how did his answer make her feel?

JAKE HAD BEEN thinking about asking out Hannah since the day they had met, but she was a hard person for him to read. He hadn't missed her hesitation when he had suggested dinner. Maybe she thought he was rushing things, inviting her to his apartment instead of to a public place.

But she had said yes and was with him now, climbing the stairs to his apartment. "Are your parents expecting you?" he asked as he unlocked the door. "Will they worry?"

"I'll text them." She pulled out her phone. "It's not as if they deliberately keep tabs on my comings and goings, but they would probably worry." She typed for a few seconds, then pocketed the phone.

He pushed open the door and Gus barreled in ahead of them. The dog snatched up a stuffed duck and brought it to Hannah. "Is that your toy?" she cooed. "Do you want me to play?"

While she tussled with the dog, Jake made a quick pass through the living room, gathering coffee cups and random shoes and stashing them in the kitchen and his bedroom. When he returned to the living room, Hannah was standing in front of his bookcase, studying the titles.

"It's mostly law enforcement stuff," he said.

"So I see. I don't think I'll be asking to borrow *Practical Homicide Investigation* anytime soon."

"I read fiction," he said. "But it's mostly ebooks."

"Oh, me too," she said. "I'm always grateful for books on my phone when I'm stuck waiting somewhere." She turned to survey the rest of the room. "Nice place."

Though small, the one-bedroom apartment featured high ceilings, full-length windows and hardwood floors. "There's a plaque downstairs that says the building was constructed in

1910," he said. "I think originally the shop owners lived here."

"You were lucky to get it," she said. "Rentals are scarce around here."

"You mentioned that's one reason you live at the inn."

"I used to have my own place," she said. "I moved back home when my mom was diagnosed with cancer."

He opened his mouth to say he was sorry to hear that, but she cut him off. "She's fine now, but I needed to be close while she was undergoing treatment. Then they lost a couple of longtime employees and I started filling in." She shrugged. "It's just easier this way. We turned one of the guest suites into a little efficiency apartment for me. It's not as nice as this, but the price is right."

"Let's go in the kitchen and see what I can find to eat," he said.

The kitchen was small, but modern, with quartz counters and black stainless appliances. Hannah pulled out one of the black iron bar stools and sat at the small island. "I'm not picky," she said. "But I am hungry."

He opened the refrigerator and surveyed the contents. Eggs, tomatoes, onion— "How about shakshuka?" he asked.

"Will you think I'm a dope if I admit I don't know what that is?" she asked.

"Poached eggs in tomatoes and onions," he said.

"Sounds good," she said.

"It's fast, too," he said, pulling ingredients from the refrigerator. "We can talk while I cook."

"Where did you learn to cook?" she asked.

He switched on the oven and slid in a half loaf of French bread he pulled from the pantry. "My mom. She was big on teaching her kids to be self-sufficient. My two sisters and I were each responsible for dinner one night a week." He pulled several jars of spices from the cabinet.

"Smart woman," Hannah said.

"Both my parents are pretty sharp." He began chopping tomatoes.

"Can I do anything to help?"

"No. This won't take long. Tell me how you came to be a paramedic."

"First, you tell me how you ended up in law enforcement."

"My father never said, but he would have liked it if I stayed on to run the ranch," he said. "But I saw how hard they worked, how much debt they carried and how they were at the mercy of so many things that were out of their control— weather and commodity prices and competition from foreign markets. I wanted something more stable. I went to college to study economics and thought I'd work in a bank."

She tried, and failed, to stifle a bark of laughter. "Sorry," she said. "I'm just having a hard time picturing you as a banker."

"Yeah, well, I figured out pretty quickly that I would be bored silly working in a bank. So I was looking around for something else when I met a law enforcement recruiter at a campus career fair. I attended a citizen's police academy, did some ride-alongs. I was hooked and I ended up enrolling in the state's police academy after I graduated college."

"What was it that hooked you?" she asked.

"The job is never routine. You have to be independent and think on your feet. And it's a real rush, helping people. I like the problem solving. I even like the training." He started dicing the onion and garlic. "I want to learn more, to get better at my job and move up the ranks so that one day, things will be better for my family."

"And you think there's more opportunity with highway patrol," she said.

He moved to the stove and switched on a burner, and drizzled olive oil in a pan. "I know there is. The starting salary there is more than deputies who have been here three years make.

And I can branch out to criminal investigation or a drug task force—all kinds of things."

"I guess that makes sense," she said.

He added the onions and garlic to the pan. "Your turn. Why a paramedic?"

"I was going to be a veterinarian," she said. "Until I found out how many years of schooling that took and how much it cost. I was working in a T-shirt shop downtown when my mom got sick. She had a rough time of it with some of her early treatment and we had the paramedics at the inn several times. I got to know some of them and they let me know about a program the town has to pay for the training if you agree to a three-year contract."

"And you like the work." He added tomatoes to the pan and fragrant steam rose.

"I do. Like you said—it's a rush to help people. And I discovered I'm really calm in a crisis, which helps."

"So how did you end up with Search and Rescue?" he asked.

"At the time, I was the only paramedic who wasn't part of the group," she said. "They guilted me into joining, but I ended up loving it. I stayed even after the rest of them moved on. I liked testing myself physically and mentally. And with all the training, I'm in the best shape of my life."

He grinned. "I hadn't noticed."

She laughed and he joined her. "I know you're not doing it just for the exercise," he said. "It's a big commitment to help people who are mostly strangers."

"It is." She slid off the stool and came to stand beside him. "But now that I'm part of the team, they're like my family. We all depend on each other and we're all working for something bigger than ourselves."

He nodded and took an egg from the carton. "Law enforcement is like that, too."

She watched as he cracked four eggs into the pan, then set the lid on. "Those need to cook for a few minutes. I don't have any wine, but I probably have time to go down the street to the liquor store."

"Water is fine," she said.

He set plates, silverware and glasses in front of the two barstools, then checked the eggs. "Almost done," he said, and switched off the heat.

They made comfortable small talk while they ate. Gus lay on the floor between them, sad brown eyes fixed on them. "I'm really glad you kept him," Hannah said as she rubbed the dog with the toe of her shoe. "It's probably just as well I didn't go to vet school—I would have taken in every homeless pet I came across."

"I didn't realize how much I missed having a

dog until Gus came along." He dropped a bite of egg and the dog snatched it up.

She fell silent and when he looked over he realized she wasn't looking at him or the dog anymore, but somewhere in the distance. "What is it?" he asked.

She shook her head. "It's not exactly polite dinner conversation."

He pushed his plate away. "We've eaten everything," he said. "So tell me."

She took a deep breath. "It's Charlie Cutler. Do you really think he's staying in the area because of me?"

"We don't know," he said. "Really, we don't. He may be staying here because he doesn't have anywhere to go. Or maybe he enjoys toughing it out in the wilderness, getting the better of the small-town cops."

"You said you read his file. You said he picked out his victims ahead of time and stalked them?"

"He observed them long enough to learn their routines," he said. "But he can't do that with you. He can't risk coming into town where you live. Someone would notice him. Eagle Mountain is too small and we've made sure his picture is everywhere."

She nodded. The fire station had one of the sheriff's department posters, with Cutler's photo, on the front door, as did the library. Even her parents had tacked one to the bulletin board in the breakfast area of the inn.

"The thing is," she said, "he can keep tabs on me when I go on calls in the area. By now he knows I'm with Search and Rescue. Maybe he even knows I'm a volunteer. Maybe he killed Al Grantham so Search and Rescue could respond and he'd have a chance to watch me."

He covered her hand with his own—her fingers were ice-cold. "Cutler killed Alan Grantham in order to steal his winter clothing and skis," Jake said. "Having those things greatly increased his chances of survival."

She nodded. "Of course." She didn't move her hand away, and he became more aware of the softness of her skin, of the delicate structure of bones beneath his hand and the herbal scent of her hair cutting through the savory aromas of their dinner. He tried to think of something to say to ease her mind.

"The other women Cutler fixated on didn't know he was after them," he said. "They didn't have a chance to take precautions, to vary their routine or make sure they were always with other people. You have that advantage over them, and I think it's a big one."

She nodded, and turned up her hand to lace her fingers with his. "You're right. And when

I am on a call, I've got the whole SAR team watching out for me."

"And you've got me," he said. His gaze shifted to her lips. He wanted to kiss her, but wasn't sure if now was the time.

She looked away, a faint blush warming her cheeks. "Thanks for dinner," she said, slipping her hand from beneath his and standing. "Let me help you with the dishes."

He fed Gus, then she washed while he dried, but the breeziness they had enjoyed when she had first arrived had given way to a different energy, an awareness that buzzed between them as they brushed against each other, then pulled away, or locked eyes, then quickly averted gazes. It was a tantalizing game of keep-away.

The last dish done, Hannah dried her hands and turned to him. "I'd better go," she said. "Thanks again for a lovely evening."

"I should be thanking you," he said. "This beat eating in front of the TV by a mile." He followed her to the coat hooks by the door. "Let me walk you to your car."

The dog whined and pawed at his leg. "Correction. Gus and I will walk you to your car."

The night was clear, a wash of stars glittering against the blackness overhead. The sharp cold burned their cheeks and Hannah shoved her gloved hands deep into the pockets of her parka. "Beautiful night," he said, though he was looking at her when he spoke.

She nodded. "You should see the high country at night. There's zero light pollution and the number of stars is amazing. I sometimes look at them when I'm on a Search and Rescue call and I'm trying to take my mind off how cold and tired I am."

"Do you have to go on a lot of night calls?"

"More so in the summer," she said. "It can take a while to locate lost hikers, or even to get to a person who's been injured at high elevation. Sometimes we have to bring them down in the dark, or on a few rare occasions, wait for enough light for a helicopter to airlift them out. Looking at the stars and picking out constellations helps to pass the time."

"You really are amazing," he said.

They reached her car and she hit the button on the key fob to release the locks. "Not amazing," she said. "Just too stubborn to give up." He reached up and brushed his cheek with the tips of her fingers. "Thanks again," she said.

"Can I kiss you good night?" he asked.

"Oh yes."

He slid one arm around to pull her closer, and pressed his lips to hers. Soft and pliant, warm and sweet, the sensation spreading through him. She moved closer, shaping her body to his, and he deepened the kiss, the sweep of her tongue across his lips sending a fresh jolt of heat through him. He lost himself in that kiss, and would have gladly stood there with her for hours, but Gus grew impatient and tugged at the leash.

Reluctantly, Jake broke the contact and lifted his head to stare into her eyes, which looked back at him, dark and a little sleepy with desire. She stepped back, smiling, and opened the door of her car. "Good night," she said.

He waited until she drove away before he started walking back across the park. It had been a good night. The first of what he hoped would be many others.

Chapter Ten

Jake was leaving Kate's Café at lunch mid-week when he almost collided with highway patrol Officer Phil Landers. "Hey, Jake, how's it going?" Landers said.

"Good, Phil. How are you?" Jake moved away from the door to the restaurant and unfastened Gus's leash from the bench on the sidewalk. The dog greeted him enthusiastically.

"I'm great," Phil said. "Good-looking dog. Is he yours?"

"This is Gus." Jake patted the dog, then straightened. "What have you been up to?"

"A lot. I'm glad I ran into you before I left town. You won't be seeing me around here anymore. I'm transferring to Denver."

"That's a good thing, I hope," Jake said.

"Oh yeah. A promotion, actually. Like I told you, there's lots of opportunity for advancement in state patrol. Have you put in your application yet?"

"I thought I'd wait until I'd been on the job here a little longer."

"I'd do it now, get your name in line. You never know when something is going to open up."

"I'll think about it," Jake said. "Good luck in Denver." Phil went into the restaurant and Jake continued down the sidewalk, back toward the office. Should he put in an application with state patrol? He had planned to stay in Eagle Mountain another year or two, at least, to gain more experience. Would the state even want an officer who was still so green?

It would be better to wait, he decided. Plus, he really liked Eagle Mountain. He was just settling in, getting to know the area and the people.

Getting to know Hannah Richards. She'd been a little standoffish at first, but he felt like they were really getting along now. Dinner with her the other night had been special, and the kiss they had shared after he walked her to her car had held the promise of more. He wanted to stick around and see what developed there.

Lost in thought, he didn't hear the man calling his name at first. Tony Meissner had to step in front of him to get his attention. "Just the person I wanted to see," Tony said when Jake stopped on the sidewalk outside the sheriff's department.

"What can I do for you, Tony?" Jake ordered Gus to sit and the dog obeyed. He was definitely getting better.

"Search and Rescue is conducting a training exercise up in Galloway Basin Sunday," Tony said. "I thought you might like to join us."

"Any particular reason you want me there?" Jake asked. Were they worried about Charlie Cutler?

"I'm hoping you'll like it enough you'll decide to sign on as a volunteer," Tony said. "We're always looking for new people, and having a deputy on the roster could come in handy sometimes."

"It sounds interesting," Jake said.

"It is. And you'll learn skills that could be useful in your regular job, too," Tony said. "You get to spend time out of doors with a bunch of great people, and help the community."

"Sure. I'll come to the training," Jake said. He would get to see Hannah, just one more reason to participate.

"Nine o'clock, at the parking area on the highway," Tony said. "You'll see all the cars. Dress for a day out of doors."

Tony left and Jake pushed open the door to the sheriff's department, Gus at his heels. While Jake turned down the hallway to head to his desk, Gus stopped by Adelaide's desk, where the dog knew the office manager kept a box of biscuits for him. Though she claimed not to approve of the dog, she kept her desk stocked with goodies for him, and had even presented him with a bandanna printed with the sheriff's department logo. "Now he looks like he belongs with the department," she had said as she tied the bandanna around his neck.

Biscuit eaten, Gus joined Jake at his desk, where a note in Adelaide's handwriting instructed him to "see the sheriff." Jake ordered Gus to stay and walked the few feet to Travis's office. Travis looked up when Jake tapped on the door. "Jake, come in."

Jake entered. He wondered if he would ever get over the feeling of being called into the principal's office when he was singled out by his boss like this. "I wanted to let you know you may be hearing from the FBI," Travis said. "They've taken an interest in Charlie Cutler."

"Yes, sir." Jake wasn't surprised the feds would be part of the search for a fugitive wanted in two states.

"I notified the regional office as soon as Cutler escaped in our territory," Travis said. "I was hoping they'd kick in on the search but I didn't hear anything until this morning." His expression was as stoic as ever, but Jake thought he detected a note of disdain in the sheriff's voice.

"If an agent calls you, give him whatever information he needs. I've already let them know we haven't had much to go on. We're trying to check all the backcountry properties Cutler might be using as shelter, but a lot of them are accessible only by snowmobile this time of year and we don't have the personnel to check them all. I suggested the FBI might send some people to help, but I didn't get the impression they thought that was necessary."

"Does Cutler have any contacts in this area?" Jake asked. "Friends or family who might help him out?"

"Not that I know of," Travis said. "According to his file, his family are all in Utah."

"Not that far away, as the crow flies," Jake said.

"The FBI hinted that they think that's where Cutler was headed when he escaped."

"But he didn't leave," Jake said. "I don't think it's because he couldn't. He's already demonstrated he has the skills to survive, even thrive, under harsh conditions."

"He stayed because he likes the way he's living now," Travis said. "Or he enjoys taunting local law enforcement. Or because he's fixated on his next victim."

"Hannah Richards." The words tasted bitter. "Has Hannah reported anything unusual since that bandanna was left on her car?" Travis asked. "Do you think she would tell us if she had?"

"I think she would tell us. Cutler really frightened her. But she hasn't said anything. Maybe he's focused on someone or something else now."

"I don't like playing guessing games with him," Travis said. "We're not going to let our guard down. If you talk to the FBI, make sure they know that, too."

"Yes, sir." Jake returned to his desk, mind churning. He had read through Cutler's file again, searching for any clue about what the murderer might be up to. He was beginning to think that in order to catch criminals, he needed to learn to think like a criminal—an unsettling realization.

SUNDAY MORNING, the SAR team assembled in the parking area near Galloway Basin, a popular backcountry skiing area, for field training. A storm had moved in during the night and it was still snowing when they arrived, with occasional gusts of wind sending the snow swirling around them or blowing hard pellets of ice straight at them. "Did you order this weather just for us?" Ted asked Tony as they gathered in front of their parked vehicles.

"It's perfect weather for our training today," Tony said. "The topic is winter wilderness first aid. We're going to be practicing assessment and treatment, with an emphasis on some problems particular to winter, such as hypothermia and frostbite, as well as practice some techniques for transport over snow and ice. Ah, and we have a new volunteer with us today."

The others turned to see Jake striding toward them. "Hello." He nodded to the group in general, and smiled when his gaze locked with Hannah's.

"Deputy Gwynn asked to join our training today, as he thought it might be useful in his work as a deputy," Tony said.

"Please, call me Jake."

"All right, Jake," Tony said. "I assume you're certified in basic first aid and CPR."

"Yes, sir," Jake said.

"Then you can start us out with that section of the training. Austen, get our Resusci Anne out here."

Austen hauled the CPR dummy dressed in the bright Hawaiian shirt out of the back of Tony's SUV and arranged her on the packed snow in front of the parking area. "We'll start with solo CPR," Tony said.

Jake knelt in front of the dummy and went through the protocol of checking for a pulse, opening the airway and beginning chest compressions. Above him, Tony talked about the procedure. "Jake is doing the standard of thirty chest compressions and two rescue breaths. Ideally, he would continue to do this until help arrived. In the real world, we know that help could take an hour or more to get to him." He consulted the stopwatch in his hand. "You're at one minute, Jake."

Jake nodded and continued. He was breathing hard now, but kept going.

"If we're on a call as a team, we don't have to depend on one person to administer CPR," Tony said. "Someone starts, and someone else takes over when the first rescuer begins to fatigue. You'd probably have a pair trading off performing chest compressions and rescue breathing." He studied the stopwatch and after a long interval—during which the sound of Jake's efforts were loud in the snowy silence—Tony called, "Okay, you can stop now, Jake."

Jake sat back, panting. "What did you notice about this exercise?" Tony asked.

"I'm pretty winded," Jake said.

"We're at eleven thousand feet here," Tony said. "Less oxygen and even for someone in good physical condition, CPR is strenuous. Not only are you winded, but what you probably didn't notice was that your chest compressions were not going as deep as they need to in order to be most effective. A 2014 study in the *American Journal of Emergency Medicine* reported that the quality of chest compressions began to decline after only thirty seconds at altitude, and continued to decline, even if the rescuers did not report feeling fatigued. So what's the takeaway?"

"If you've got more than one person able to perform CPR, switch off more often," Danny said.

"Yes," Tony said. "Carrie, you and Danny get down here and switch off every other set of compressions."

As Danny and Carrie took his place, Jake moved over beside Hannah. She hadn't seen him since their dinner a week ago—and their kiss by her car. "You didn't tell me you were thinking of joining SAR," she whispered as Carrie and Danny demonstrated the awkward quick transition.

"All right, Austen, you come in here and let's work with three people in a relay setup," Tony said.

"I ran into Tony in town earlier in the week and he suggested I might want to participate in some of the training," Jake said. "He'd like to have a law enforcement person as part of the regular team."

"I can see how that would be useful sometimes," she said.

The CPR demonstration ended and they moved on to risk assessment for both patients and rescuers, diagnosing and treating frostbite and hypothermia. "Let's talk about warming techniques," Tony said. "Hannah, come be the victim."

Hannah joined Tony at the front of the group. He instructed her to lie down, then discussed the methods of assessing hypothermia in the field. All of this was information they had reviewed in the classroom previously, but standing in the mountains with snow swirling around them made the challenges of the assessment more real.

They discussed handling and treating various levels of hypothermia, with and without other injuries or conditions. All Hannah had to do was lie still while Tony, assisted at various times by Ted or Ryan, demonstrated various procedures.

"All right," Tony said, when the discussion of hypothermia was concluded. "Let's move out a little and we're going to practice patient transport in both stable and unstable snow conditions."

Hannah rejoined Jake. "It's a lot to remember," he said.

"And we get tested on this stuff, so get ready to study," she said.

The team members strapped on snowshoes and followed Tony about a half mile from the group, each carrying some piece of equipment, from ropes to a plastic litter, and various first aid equipment. They walked in single file, packing down a trail that could be used when coming back out with an injured person or persons.

They reached the area Tony had selected for the exercise and spread out. "What are those buildings up there?" Jake pointed up the slope to a cluster of ruins.

"That's the Jack of Hearts Mine," Danny said. "Or what's left of it."

For the next hour Tony laid out various possible rescue scenarios and they discussed the best approaches, then practiced those approaches, taking turns being the victims and the rescuers. It took real physical effort and strength to move the weight of an injured person, plus any supplies used in treating them, over rough terrain in wind and snow, plummeting temperatures and thin air.

By the time Tony signaled the break for lunch, everyone was winded and chilled. "Let's head up to the mine and get out of this wind," Danny said.

"I'd like to see it," Jake said. He turned to Hannah. "Do you want to come?"

She had been looking forward to sitting in her car with the heater running, but shrugged. "Sure. Why not?"

"We'll have to approach from the east to avoid that cornice on the west side," Danny said. "With all this snow dumping, it's liable to be unstable." Hannah and Jake followed him along a ridge that led away from the mine, then back through a wooded area to what he told them was an old Jeep road. The long hike in snowshoes warmed Hannah, so by the time they reached the mine site, she was feeling more enthusiastic about exploring the place.

The mine site consisted of a couple of small cabins and one larger building. The cabins were little more than piles of logs and tin, but the larger building, though gutted inside, still had four intact outer walls and a solid, though rust-ing, roof. Danny led the way to the door, kick-ing aside the snow until they could push open the heavy door and tramp inside.

All of the windows in the building were bro-ken or missing, and at some point the openings had been boarded, but someone had ripped the plywood from one of the larger openings, letting in enough light for the three of them to see most of the interior. Large pieces of rusting metal—

what must have been an old woodstove—lay scattered in the back corner of the building.

Danny kicked off his snowshoes and walked over to one of these. He nudged at a pile of charred wood and ash with the toe of his boot. "Someone's had a fire here," he said. "And not that long ago, from the looks of it."

Hannah could smell the smoke now. "I didn't notice any woodsmoke smell on the way here," she said.

"The wind was blowing it away from us," Danny said.

Jake moved over beside him, and crouched down to hold his hand over the remains of the campfire. "The coals are still warm," he said.

"That trash isn't antique, either." Danny pointed to an empty can that had once held chili, and a flattened cracker box.

A shiver raced up Hannah's spine. "Do you think it was Charlie Cutler?" she asked. Who else would be camping out here in February?

"Maybe." Jake straightened and began examining the rest of the cabin. Hannah looked up at the second floor of the building. So much of the flooring was missing that she could see all the way to the underside of the metal roof. But was there enough flooring left for Cutler to be hiding up there, looking down on them?

"If he was here, I think he's gone now." Jake

stood in the opening of what would have been the back door. The door itself hung from one rusting hinge at an acute angle. Jake pointed out the opening and Hannah moved in behind him and looked at the ski tracks headed away from the cabin.

"Those couldn't have been made more than a few minutes ago," Danny said from behind her. "It's snowing hard enough, they would have been covered otherwise."

"He was just here," Hannah whispered.

"You don't know it was Cutler," Danny said. "The parking lot is full of cars. Maybe someone else was up here, having lunch and warming up."

"How many people come up here by themselves?" she asked. "If they do, they're not being very smart."

Danny shrugged. "That doesn't mean those tracks are Cutler's."

Jake had turned away from the door and was investigating the rest of the cabin. He paused at the front door. "It was Cutler," he said. "He left us a message."

Hannah and Danny hurried to join him. The door, hewn from fir logs and darkened with age, was crisscrossed with graffiti of all kinds, but at eye level a new message had been gouged deep into the wood, the letters bright against the dark boards: CC <3 HR.

CHARLIE CUTLER LOVES *HANNAH RICHARDS*.

"You don't know that's what those initials mean," Danny said when Jake voiced his suspicions. "They could stand for Chris Carson and Heidi Rogers."

"Who are Chris Carson and Heidi Rogers?" Hannah asked. Though pale, she remained calm.

"I don't know," Danny said. "I made the names up. I'm just saying that those initials could be anybody."

"They could," Jake agreed. "But I don't think they are."

"How would he even know Hannah's name?" Danny asked.

"I think I introduced myself, when I saw him right after the accident," she said.

Jake returned to the back door and stared out at the ski tracks—or where the ski tracks had been. The fast-falling snow had already mostly covered them.

"You can't go after him." Hannah spoke from just behind him. He had been so engrossed in staring in the direction the tracks had disappeared that he hadn't heard her approach.

He glanced back at her. "He could be very close," he said.

"And he has skis and at least one gun—maybe more. If he really has been watching me, then he knows who you are, too. He knows you're one of the deputies who's been hunting him. He's already killed one cop. Why would he even think twice about killing you?"

He nodded. "I won't try to go after him." Not alone, for all the reasons she had named, and for another—he wouldn't leave her alone, knowing Cutler could be nearby.

"We need to get back to the others," Danny said. "Tony is going to give us grief for being gone so long."

"I'll need to drive to where I can call this in," Jake said. His phone wasn't getting a signal here.

"We haven't eaten lunch yet," Hannah said. "Not that any of this has improved my appetite, but we've burned a lot of energy this morning and it's not smart to be out in the cold and hungry if you can help it."

"So we eat and move at the same time," Danny said. He looked around. "I'm man enough to admit I'm a little spooked and I'd just as soon get out of here."

"Yeah, me too," Hannah said.

"Then let's go," Danny said.

They donned their snowshoes again and set out. Hannah dug in her pack and pulled out her lunch. "Peanut butter?" Jake asked, catching the scent as she bit into the sandwich.

"Hey, it keeps well, it doesn't matter if it gets crushed or cold or hot, and I happen to like it." She took a bite. "What are you eating?"

"Summer sausage, cheese sticks, nuts and an apple."

"All good trail food," she said. "You get an A on the food portion of wilderness training."

"Extra credit for dessert," Danny said. He pulled a large Snickers bar from the pocket of his jacket. "Chocolate, nuts and sugar. Perfect energy food."

"I see your candy and raise you cookies." Jake brandished a large oatmeal cookie.

Both men looked to Hannah. "I could go with either," she said. She plunged a hand into her pocket and drew out a bright yellow package. "I'm a peanut M&M's woman, myself."

"Not your mother's brownies?" Danny asked, sounding disappointed.

"Not today."

Danny clapped Jake on the shoulder. "You haven't lived until you've tasted one of Brit's brownies," he said. "She bakes them for all the SAR fundraisers and they always sell out."

The sudden camaraderie surprised Jake. He had gotten the impression before that Danny resented him—whether it was because the other man didn't like law enforcement or perhaps was jealous of Jake's ill-concealed interest in Hannah, he hadn't been able to tell. But maybe it was just a veteran's natural resentment of a newcomer to a tight-knit group like Search and Rescue. Maybe at the training today Jake had managed to earn a little respect and acceptance.

They moved out of the wooded portion of the hike and began to make their way down the hill toward the parking area. The snow had let up somewhat and the sun even showed signs of peeking through. "It figures the weather would improve when we only have a couple more hours of training," Danny said.

"Be careful what you wish for," Hannah said. "If the weather turns too good, people will want to get out in the fresh snow and the chances of someone making a mistake and triggering a slide go up."

"If they do, at least we'll be close," Danny said. "Unless, of course, they're on the other side of the county."

"You know they will be," she said, and laughed.

The sound released a tension in Jake he hadn't even recognized he had been holding in. The sight of those initials carved on the cabin door had solidified his theory that Cutler had fixated on Hannah. He had worried that truth would terrify her. But maybe it only confirmed something she had learned to live with. It didn't mean she wasn't afraid, but she wasn't letting that reality defeat her.

Then again, he should have realized a woman who regularly risked her life to save others wouldn't frighten easily. "What are we going to cover this afternoon?" he asked. Depending on what the sheriff decided about pursuing Cutler, he might have time to take in at least part of the afternoon training before another law enforcement search team convened at the mine.

Danny turned to answer him, then his eyes widened and he swore—loudly. Jake whipped around to see what had caught his attention and added his own curse. With a sound like whitewater rapids, snow cascaded down the slope to the west of the mine site. Snow rose in clouds and re-formed into waves, ripping down the mountain, tearing up trees by the roots and tossing them up like twigs.

"Carrie!" Hannah's scream rose over the sound of the avalanche, and Jake's gaze shifted to take in two people in the path of the snowslide, both in the bright yellow parkas that were part of the search and rescue group's uniform, one short and one tall. As he watched in horror, they disappeared in a wave of snow.

Chapter Eleven

Hannah took off running, snowshoes slapping awkwardly, pack bouncing on her back. Danny caught up with her, then passed her, and they joined the others in running toward the slide path. Tony was barking orders, directing them where to search while he and Ted set their transceivers to receive signals from Carrie's and Ryan's units.

"Over here!" Austen shouted, and they converged, quickly, but carefully, on a section of the slide. Already the snow had set like concrete, and they attacked the snow with shovels, hacking at it with all the force they could muster. Hannah moved back to let the others dig, and did a mental inventory of the medical supplies in her SUV and what she knew Danny and Tony carried in their vehicles. They had plenty of stretchers and splints, supplemental oxygen, bandages...

"I'm okay! I'm okay! Find Ryan!" Carrie

shouted as Austen and Ted hauled her from the snow. She protested as they moved in to examine her. "I'm fine. I've taken worse falls on my mountain bike. Just find Ryan."

"We've got Ryan!" Danny called.

Ryan was less ebullient than Carrie, and emerged cradling his left arm. Hannah moved in and she and Danny examined him. "If it's broken, I don't think it's a bad break," Hannah said. "But you'll need an X-ray to be sure."

"I'm betting it's just a bad sprain," Danny said.

"That better be all it is," Ryan said. "I'm supposed to compete in ice climbing in two weeks."

"Two weeks might be a little soon," Hannah said.

His answer was a growl of frustration. She and Danny walked with him to rejoin the others. Carrie had removed her knit cap and was brushing snow from her hair with her fingers. "Good thing we were at the very bottom of the slide when it let loose," she said, looking back up the slope. "I thought we were low enough we were safe, but I guess I was wrong."

"I thought I saw someone up there," Ted said. "I caught a flash of blue just before everything came down. I was about to yell to the guy that he was stupid to be up there."

"He wouldn't have heard you," Carrie said. "Not all the way up there."

"I'd like to find whoever it was and shake some sense into him." Ryan rubbed at his arm. "I think you're right," he said to Danny. "I don't think my arm is broken."

"Whoever was up there could have been caught in the slide," Tony said.

"I don't think so," Hannah said. "I saw everything from the first and there was no one else caught."

"I agree," Danny said. "If someone set this off, they were above the slide itself—out of danger, but a danger to others."

"The ski parka Charlie Cutler stole from Al Grantham was blue," Jake said.

The others turned to stare at him. He had stayed back while the others searched, letting them do the work they were trained for. But now he rejoined them. "You think this was Cutler?" Tony asked.

"When Hannah and Danny and I went up to the mine at lunch, we found signs that Cutler had been there," Jake said. "Very recently."

"He had just left when we got there," Danny said. "We could see his ski tracks out the back door, and you know how hard it was snowing then. He must have left just as we were approaching. He'd had a fire in there and it was still warm." He glanced at Jake. "If it was Cutler."

"Do you think he set off that slide deliberately?" Tony asked.

"Maybe," Jake said.

"But why?" Carrie asked. Then she shook her head. "What am I saying? He's killed several people. Maybe he just likes putting others in danger."

"Maybe," Jake said, but something in his voice made Hannah look at him more closely. He looked…guarded. As if he was trying to hide something—from all of them, or just from her?

"We all need to leave the area," Jake said. "I've got to drive to where I can call this in, and we'll probably pick up the search for Cutler here." He turned to Tony. "I'm sorry to disrupt your training."

"I think we've had enough for today." He turned to the others. "You heard what the man said. Let's pack it up and go home."

"Danny, will you go with Hannah and see that she gets safely home?" Jake asked. "All the way home?"

"You bet," Danny said.

Hannah wanted to protest but she saw the sense in what Jake was asking. If Cutler really was targeting her—and it looked more and more as if he was—then she shouldn't be alone in any place where he might get to her.

She helped the others to gather equipment and load it in Tony's SUV. Danny, who had ridden to the training with Ryan, walked with Hannah to her Subaru. She hit the key fob to unlock the doors, then froze at the sight of something yellow caught beneath the rear wiper blade.

"What's that M&M's packet doing underneath your wiper blade?" Danny asked.

He reached for the packet, but she put out a hand to stop him. "Don't touch it," she said. "Not until Jake has seen it."

Danny stared at her. "Are you okay?"

She shook her head. "I think…" She swallowed, trying to manufacture enough saliva in her suddenly bone-dry mouth to speak. "I think Cutler left that," she said. "It's why he set off the avalanche, so he'd have time to leave this for me."

Was it a taunt? A threat? Or Cutler's idea of a love note? She clutched her stomach, willing herself not to be sick right here in the parking lot. She was ready for this to be over. Now.

JAKE FELT SICK to his stomach as he stared at the candy wrapper stuck beneath Hannah's wiper blade, a warning flag that Cutler had been this close. "How do you think he got hold of it?" he asked Hannah. He tried to keep his voice calm, not wanting to add to her fears, though he could see she was pale and shaky.

"I must have dropped it when the avalanche happened," she said. "The last thing I was thinking about then was litter."

He nodded and looked at the others who had gathered around. "We all need to leave the area right away." He looked past them, to the few skiers who had gathered, probably drawn by the outcry. "I'm with the sheriff's department," he said, raising his voice. "I'm closing this area immediately. You all need to leave at once."

A few people started to protest, but Tony turned and addressed them. "You heard the man! Everyone needs to get out of here. It's not safe."

"Thanks," Jake said.

"I'll stay and help you make sure everyone clears out," Tony said.

"Carrie, will you and Danny stay with Hannah?" Jake asked. "Make sure she gets back to the Alpiner Inn. Don't leave until you're sure she's inside with her parents."

"We'll take care of her." Carrie put her arm around Hannah's shoulders.

"I'm sorry, but you'll need to leave your car here for now," Jake said to Hannah. "I'll make sure you get it back as soon as possible."

She nodded, her eyes glazed. Jake moved in closer and took her gloved hands in his. "You're safe," he said. "And I'm going to make sure it stays that way."

Her eyes met his, and the fear in them sent anger burning through him. He hated Cutler for making her feel this way—for transforming the strong, lively woman of this morning into this trembling, fearful one.

Gradually the area emptied out. Hannah left with Carrie and Danny. Tony stayed with Jake until the last of the skiers had driven away and the only vehicles left in the lot were Hannah's Subaru, Tony's SUV and Jake's personal Jeep. The two of them set up barricades to close off the lot. "What's this guy Cutler playing at?" Tony asked.

"I don't know," Jake said.

"I heard he'd killed a bunch of women. Is he after Hannah?"

"He could be," Jake said. "That's the second time he's left something on her car. Or at least, we think he's the one who left the items." He didn't mention the graffiti in the cabin. No one else needed to know about that.

"We'll all keep an eye on her," Tony said. "She's special. We don't want anything to happen to her."

Jake nodded. Hannah was special. Maybe that

was what drew Cutler to her. He saw that quality in her and for some reason wanted to extinguish it.

He left the parking area right behind Tony, and hit the siren coming off the pass, racing toward the sheriff's department. He called the sheriff on the way in and gave him a summary of what had happened. "I'll call out the search teams," Travis said. "Maybe we'll get lucky and be able to track him in the fresh snow."

"Can we get eyes in the air?" Jake asked. A helicopter might be able to spot something searchers couldn't.

"I'll try," Travis said. "But we only have a couple of hours of daylight left. I doubt we have time to mobilize a chopper."

Travis didn't mention his budget, but Jake knew that was a consideration, too. Air support cost hundreds, if not thousands, of dollars an hour, and the department had already spent a small fortune on the hunt for Charlie Cutler.

An hour later, he was back on the mountain, in a line of officers spreading out in all directions from the parking lot and the Jack of Hearts Mine. There were plenty of ski tracks in the area, but they had no way of knowing which ones belonged to Cutler. They also had a high avalanche danger to contend with.

A forensics team searched the mine buildings

and collected a few items, and examined the exterior of Hannah's car. "There's really nothing there," Gage reported when they gathered at the sheriff's department much later that night. By then the search had been called because of darkness and another snowstorm blowing in.

They reviewed everything that had happened that day, and everything they knew, but it all added up to a big nothing. Cutler had vanished into the wilderness again. They knew he was still in the area, and he was apparently focused on Hannah. "The next move is up to him," Travis said. "As hard as it is, all we can do is wait."

Jake was exhausted by the time he left the office, but too keyed up to sleep. It was after eleven. Too late to bother Hannah and her parents, but he drove to the Alpiner Inn anyway. The front door was locked and a sign said to ring the bell if you needed assistance. He hesitated, and peered in the window, trying to see if anyone was in the lobby.

Thad Richards opened the door. He looked ten years older, dark circles beneath his eyes, his tall frame hunched. "Jake! Is everything all right? Has Cutler—"

"We haven't found him," Jake said. "I just wanted to check on Hannah. How is she doing?"

"Her mother persuaded her to take a sleeping pill and go to bed. Then Brit did the same. Both of them were worn-out."

"You look beat yourself," Jake said.

"I am, but someone had to stay up. Come in. I just made some hot chocolate. There's plenty for two."

Jake waited while Thad locked the door behind them, then followed him into a little kitchen off the lobby. "We use this for the breakfasts we serve guests," Thad explained. He opened a cabinet and pulled out a box of hot chocolate packets, then took a couple of mugs from hooks on the wall. "Have you been up on the mountain all day?"

"We searched until it wasn't safe to do so anymore," Jake said. "I think part of the problem is there are so many of us hunting for him, Cutler can see and hear us from a long way off, and he has plenty of time to get away."

"Hannah told me he set off an avalanche while the SAR team was up there." He emptied the chocolate packet into the mugs, then added water from an electric kettle. "You're lucky he didn't do the same to the searchers."

"I think he was smart enough not to try to play cat and mouse with us this evening." He accepted the mug of chocolate and took a sip. The hot, sweet drink hit him in a soothing wave and he sighed.

"I appreciate all you're doing to help Hannah," Thad said.

"I'm not doing anything," Jake said. "Not enough, anyway."

"She's been through an awful lot these last few years," Thad said. "Did she tell you she moved back home to take care of her mother when Brit had cancer?"

"She mentioned it, yes."

"Then I had my accident. The worst part of the whole thing was seeing how torn up Hannah was about it."

"She didn't say anything about you being in an accident," Jake said.

"She doesn't like to talk about it." Thad set aside his empty mug. "I fell climbing ice in Caspar Canyon three years ago. Hannah had just signed on with Search and Rescue and was on the call. She didn't know it was me until she saw me lying there on the ground. It really shook her up."

"You look like you're doing okay now."

"I can predict the weather with my joints now." He rubbed at one knee. "I healed up okay, but it was a close call. I'm sure Search and Rescue saved my life. When I saw how upset Brit and Hannah were, I promised them I'd stop competing."

"Was it hard to give it up?" Jake asked.

"Not as tough as I thought it would be. I think I was at a place in my life where I had done a lot of exciting stuff, climbed all over the world, and had a display case full of medals. It's enough for me now to stay home and climb every once in a while just for fun. And my girls are a lot happier with my decision. That means a lot. It takes a load off my mind knowing you're watching out for Hannah. I feel like she's safe with you around."

Jake wished he could be so sure.

"This Cutler guy isn't going to last out there in the mountains much longer with everyone looking for him," Thad said. "I don't care how much training he has—he's going to run out of places to break into and things to steal."

Jake didn't share Thad's confidence. Cutler had already survived on his own for a month. And it didn't matter how many more days or weeks Cutler could survive in the wilderness. He only had to make it long enough to get what he wanted. And what he wanted, apparently, was Hannah.

WORD ABOUT THE candy wrapper left on Hannah's car and its significance had spread, until she began to feel like some rare species of wild animal, everyone around watching to see what she would do next. Her mother had suggested she might like to go visit her grandparents in Oklahoma for a few weeks, her boss had offered her a leave of absence and even Tony had offered to temporarily take her off the SAR roster "until things calm down."

"What do they think I'm going to do?" she complained to Danny as the two of them sorted through the search and rescue team's medical supplies, refilling depleted items and tossing out anything that had expired. "Sit in my room with the door locked until Cutler is captured?"

"No one wants anything to happen to you." He squinted at the expiration date on a package of alcohol wipes and tossed them to one side.

"I do appreciate everyone's concern," she said. "And it's reassuring, knowing so many people are watching out for me. But it's also a little stifling." She was a strong, independent woman who climbed mountains and rappelled into canyons. She hated feeling so helpless and dependent on other people for protection.

"At least Deputy Jake is sticking close," Danny said. "It's like you have an armed bodyguard."

Hannah tossed the rolled splint she had been examining into the supply bin and stared at him. "The other day you were giving me a hard time about getting too close to Jake."

"Yeah, well, that was before I figured out

he's chiefly interested in you as a way to get to Cutler."

That certainly hadn't been her impression of Jake. When they had kissed after dinner the other night, she was pretty sure he hadn't been thinking about Cutler at all, although there hadn't been a repeat of that night. She had told herself that was because they were both so busy, but was she wrong? "What are you talking about?"

"I just put two and two together," Danny said. "He's here to beef up his résumé, wants to get on with the state cops or a bigger department. Capturing a fugitive would look great on his résumé. And that fugitive is fixated on you. So if Jake stays close to you, he ups his chances of nabbing Cutler. It's a good plan, really."

Hannah felt a little sick to her stomach. Danny had to be wrong. But he was a man. Maybe he was better at reading another man than she was. "So you don't think Jake has any romantic interest in me?"

Danny was bent over a plastic tote of supplies and his voice came out muffled. "I should have believed you when you said he didn't," he said. "But when I saw him at the training Sunday it made sense."

"What made sense?"

"That line he gave Tony about wanting to

learn skills to be a better cop—it was really just an excuse to stick close to you in the area where Cutler was known to be roaming around. It may even be why he was so eager to go check out the Jack of Hearts Mine. He probably figured it would be a good spot for Cutler to lay low, and bringing you along might lure his quarry out of hiding."

"Wait—you think Jake deliberately used me as…as *bait*?"

Danny straightened and looked at her. "Don't get upset. He wasn't going to let you get hurt. It was a good idea, really."

"It was a horrible idea. And I don't believe Jake would do such a thing." But what if she was wrong? "Did he tell you that's what he was doing?"

"No. But it just makes sense."

"More sense than that he might be interested in me?"

"Sure, he was probably attracted to you. You're cute and fun to be with. But guys figure out pretty quick when a woman isn't interested. You've made it real clear you don't want anything short-term and I'm sure he knows it."

"You seem to have spent a lot of time thinking about this."

He shrugged and went back to combing through the box of supplies. "I probably know you better than most people," he said. He fastened the lid on the box he had been sorting. "Are you done with that box?"

She looked down at the now-rearranged supplies. "Yes."

"Great. Then I'll just take this expired stuff to be boxed up at the office. Tony said we can send it to a charitable group that distributes it overseas."

Hannah stared after him as he carried the bag of expired items from the room. Obviously, Danny was wrong when he claimed to know her better than most people. If he knew anything about her at all, he would have realized she was furious with him right now.

She was gathering her things to leave when Jake walked into SAR headquarters. He had made a point to check in with her at least once a day since last Sunday, and until now she had enjoyed seeing him. She liked that he kept her informed about their search for Cutler, even though there was little real news to offer. But she felt a flash of irritation as he greeted her now.

"I need to talk to you," she said. She wasn't one to stew over suppositions when they could clear the air right now.

His smile faded. "Uh, okay."

He started to pull out a chair at the table in the

center of the room but she shook her head. She could hear Danny and Tony talking in Tony's office, and other members of the team were liable to walk in at any time. "Outside," she said. "In my car."

Jake followed her to the parking lot. His sheriff's department SUV sat in the slot next to hers and as they approached, Gus stuck his nose out the partially open window and gave an excited yip. "Hey, Gus," she said, and reached in to pat the dog.

Jake waited beside her Subaru until she unlocked it. "Is something wrong?" he asked. "You look upset."

She took her time arranging her backpack and water bottle and digging out her sunglasses, trying to choose her words. Finally, she turned to him. "Danny thinks you're sticking so close to me because you see me as your ticket to capturing Charlie Cutler and making a name for yourself."

He stared at her, mouth in a tight line.

"Well?" she said.

"I told you I was ambitious. That isn't the same as ruthless. Is that what you think of me?"

"I told him he was wrong—but is he? He said you suggested going up to the Jack of Hearts Mine because you knew it was a likely place for Cutler to be and you wanted to draw him out.

You figured if I was with you, Cutler would be more likely to surface."

He swore and looked away.

"Are you angry because Danny is wrong or because he figured you out?" she asked.

He looked back at her, face flushed, his gaze burning into her. "I'm angry that you think so little of me," he said. "That you would believe I'd use anyone that way—especially you!"

"I don't think it!" she protested. She clutched her head in her hands. "I just… This whole thing is so stressful and Danny was so sure…" Her voice trailed away. Now that she was saying all this out loud, she could hear how ridiculous it all sounded.

Jake inhaled deeply and slowly blew out the breath. "I don't know what Danny's problem is. Maybe he's jealous. I heard you two used to be a couple. Maybe he doesn't want you interested in me, so he's making sure you think I'm a bad guy."

"Danny and I agreed we weren't right for each other," she said. "He's just a friend."

"Maybe now that you're no longer together, he wants to be more than a friend."

She thought of their conversation at Mo's, when Danny had proposed they be "friends with benefits." "I don't feel that way about him," she said. "But I am pretty upset about everything that's happened. It's hard enough to figure out relationships without the pressure of a…a stalker, too."

Jake took her hand in his. "I'm sticking close because I care about you," he said. "Would I like to catch Cutler? Of course I would. Once he's caught, he won't be a threat to you any longer. As for Danny's theory that I dragged you up to that mine looking for Cutler—Danny was the one who suggested we go up there at lunch. If I had thought Cutler was up there, I would have gotten you as far away from there as I could."

She leaned toward him until their shoulders touched. "I'm sorry I accused you of putting ambition ahead of everything else," she said. "I knew even when I was hearing Danny say those things that he was wrong, but I've been so on edge and… I'm just sorry."

"It's okay." He rubbed the back of her neck, a soothing gesture, and a sensual one, too. "Will you have dinner with me tonight?" he asked.

"Yes. I'd like that." She turned her head and their lips met and she closed her eyes and relaxed into the kiss. This was what she needed right now. To forget everything but how good being in his arms felt. She needed to shut off her brain and stop debating whether Jake was right for her or wrong for her and just let herself feel something good.

And the kiss was very good. The kind of kiss she felt with her whole body, the warmth from his lips spreading through her chest to her stomach and lower, a physical reminder that while she might be threatened, she was here and alive, with a man she believed truly cared for her—a man she was growing to care for also.

A door banged in the distance, the sound startling them. They drew apart and she looked up to see Danny striding toward her. "Time to come back inside," he said, when she lowered the window. "We've got a call about a fallen climber."

Chapter Twelve

The ice climber had fallen on a steep, technical pitch in Caspar Canyon, where natural seeps and waterfalls had formed a wall of ice that attracted both professionals and amateurs from across the country. Plenty of people had been on hand when one end of the climber's rope came free, but all had been helpless to stop his plunge into the rocky gorge below.

Hannah told herself that this was just like any other call, helping someone who was injured, but as soon as she stepped out of the Beast at the entrance to the canyon, she was reminded of that day, three years ago, when her father had been the injured man. Seeing him lying there, broken and bleeding, had overwhelmed her. It was just as well that Ryan, the commander at the time, had relieved her of her duties as soon as he realized her father was the man they had been called to help.

Her dad was fine now, she reminded herself.

Completely healed, largely because Search and Rescue had gotten to him quickly, administered medical care and seen that he was transported to a trauma center, where he was wheeled into surgery a mere two hours after his fall. She had the opportunity to provide the same level of care to someone else now. She would do it for her father. The idea made her feel stronger.

The first challenge rescuers faced was getting to the injured man, who was reported to be a forty-year-old, experienced climber from Montana. He had fallen into a deeper gorge at the far end of the canyon. Sheri and another volunteer, Eldon Ramsey, rappelled one hundred feet into the gorge to assess the man and radioed their findings to Tony and the others waiting above. "I've got Brock Franklin here," Sheri said. "Mr. Franklin is conscious, but in a lot of pain. Difficulty breathing. Looks like some broken ribs, maybe a broken pelvis, probably punctured lung."

Hannah winced—"a lot of pain" didn't begin to describe what Brock Franklin was probably experiencing.

"I'm sending Hannah down with oxygen, and we'll send a litter on a separate line," Tony said.

Hannah steeled herself for the trip down. Descending rock was anxiety inducing, but slick ice made the climb down even more harrowing, not to mention cold. She reminded herself that she was attached to safety lines and had a whole team of people looking out for her. That was the thing about being part of Search and Rescue—you never had to face the difficult tasks alone.

She managed the descent with only a few jarring slips, and Eldon, a cheerful Hawaiian native who had discovered a love of ice and snow and relocated from Oahu two years before, greeted her at the bottom and helped her out of her harness. She could hear her patient moaning and gasping for breath. The same way her father had moaned and gasped. Again, she stopped to steady herself.

"Everything okay?" Eldon asked. Maybe he had heard about her father's accident, though he hadn't been with SAR then.

She nodded. "All good." She pushed the memory of her father aside and knelt beside the man. "Hello, Mr. Franklin," she said. "I'm Hannah. I'm a paramedic. I'm going to see if we can't get you breathing a little easier." She quickly assessed him, then turned to Sheri and Eldon. "I think if we reposition his head he'll be able to breathe easier."

"Let's get the neck brace on him," Eldon said.

With the man's head and neck stabilized, Hannah was able to reposition him to open his airway a little wider. That and the supplemental oxygen and some painkillers gave him a little relief. "Do you have him in the litter?" Tony radioed.

"Not yet," Sheri said. She looked to Hannah, who nodded. "We're going to move him now," Sheri radioed. "Give us a few minutes."

"Take your time," Tony said. "We've got a boom truck coming from the power company. We're going to drop a line from the boom and try to lift him straight up, but we need some time to set up everything."

Moving Franklin into the litter was a slow, excruciating process. There was no way to do so without causing the man pain, but no way to get him the help he needed without going through that pain. By the time he was secured in the aluminum litter, blankets and chemical hot packs tucked around him to make him as comfortable as possible, all three of the rescuers were sweating and chilled.

The truck from the power company had arrived and extended its boom out over the gorge, and a large crowd had gathered to watch the process. Two more volunteers descended to set anchors and guide lines, and to fasten the litter to the lines using techniques they had practiced many times but that Hannah, at least, had never used in the field. "Hannah, you need to ride the litter up with him," Tony radioed down.

"Keep the lines from getting tangled and keep him calm."

"Okay." Her brain was screaming that it really wasn't okay, but there was no other answer. Tony thought she was up to the task, so she would be up to the task.

This involved donning a harness and sling and being pulled up along with the litter. Instead of thinking about being dashed to death on the rocks if the rope snapped or the pulley failed, Hannah focused on Franklin. She put her hand on top of his body and spoke to him. "Hang in there, Brock," she said. "You're doing great. We're going to go for a quick ride and before you know it you'll be in the ambulance and on your way to help. You're a strong guy and you're going to get through this."

"Stupid mistake," he muttered. "I should have checked the rope."

"You can come back next year and do the climb right," she said, hoping she wasn't lying. They wouldn't know the true extent of his injuries until he could be examined at the hospital, but she had seen people come back from worse. Her father, for instance, though he no longer traveled the world to climb treacherous slopes in remote areas as he had done so much in his younger years.

And she had seen people die from lesser injuries, but she wasn't going to think about that now.

By the time she looked around, they were almost to the top of the gorge. The lift was so smooth she had scarcely felt it, and might have enjoyed the sensation of floating in midair in other circumstances.

Fifteen minutes later they were out of the gorge and Brock Franklin was on his way to the hospital in Junction. Checking her watch, Hannah was surprised to find that the whole rescue had taken just over three hours. "That went well," Tony said, coming up alongside her.

She nodded. "It did." Now that is was over, she could admit to feeling a little shaky, but good.

"How was the ride?" Tony asked.

"Actually, it was kind of a thrill."

He laughed. "I'll remember that, if we have to do it again." He fell into step beside her as she walked to her car. She didn't ask why he was accompanying her. Since the incident at the training Sunday, her SAR teammates had made it a point not to leave her alone at any time on a call. She appreciated their watchfulness, especially when she returned to her car. She lived in dread of finding another of Charlie Cutler's messages.

But no message awaited her this time. No

notes beneath her wiper blades, nothing left on the hood or near the car. She unlocked the vehicle and climbed in, and relief flooded her as she realized that this time, at least, Cutler had left her alone.

THE WHOLE SHERIFF'S department had lived and breathed the search for Charlie Cutler much of the last month. When Jake wasn't actively searching for the fugitive, he was reviewing Cutler's case file, searching for some clue as to his intentions and his next move, or he was checking in with Hannah to make sure she was all right. The normal duties of a sheriff's deputy in a small, rural county continued, but the usual round of barking dog complaints, traffic violations, one bar fight and a petty theft didn't demand copious amounts of time and attention, leaving Jake to fret over Cutler almost every waking hour.

When the sheriff convened a special meeting about the case, Jake hoped this meant there had been a new development—something that would lead them to finally track down and apprehend the fugitive. The first thing he noticed when he filed into the conference room with his fellow officers after leaving Hannah on Thursday was the slender man in a business suit who stood with the sheriff. "Looks like the feds finally showed up," Dwight muttered as he took his seat alongside Jake.

Jake checked out the man again. Short hair, upright posture, and no-nonsense expression. Eyes that took in everything in the room. He looked like a cop all right. "What's he doing here?" he asked Dwight.

"We're not getting anywhere on our own," Dwight said. "We need help, so maybe he's it."

The sheriff introduced the man as Special Agent Carter Sherrell with the FBI's Grand Junction office. "The FBI is assuming direction of the hunt for Charlie Cutler," Sherrell said. "We appreciate the work your department has done to this point, but we have reason to believe Cutler has left the area and is headed to Utah."

"What makes you think that?" Gage asked.

"We've interviewed Cutler's cell mate in Albuquerque and he says Cutler shared his plans to try to escape during his transport and make his way to Utah," Sherrell said. "Cutler has family and friends in the Salt Lake area he believed would hide him."

"But we have evidence that Cutler was in this area as recently as Sunday," Jake said.

Only a slight tightening of his jaw betrayed Sherrell's feelings about this question. "I've read the reports relating to the incident Sunday and the evidence for Cutler being at the scene is tentative at best. There were any number of skiers in the area who could have set off that avalanche, the graffiti on the door of the old mine building is cryptic and could stand for anything and the candy wrapper left on the female paramedic's car could have been merely an attempt by someone to chide her for littering. I find it highly unlikely that Cutler, who fled the scene of the accident the day of his escape wearing only jail coveralls and tennis shoes, could have survived the hostile conditions in that area for going on a month now."

"He stole supplies," Dwight said. "Winter clothing, food and a gun."

"Which he would need to get over the mountains to Utah," Sherrell said. "But there was no need for him to remain in such a hostile area."

"So you don't believe he remained in the area because he was focused on his next victim?" Jake asked.

The only word Jake could find to describe the FBI agent's smile was *condescending.* "We don't believe Ms. Richards was ever in any danger."

Jake wanted to believe the man, but his attitude of dismissing the on-the-ground expertise and experiences of him and his fellow officers made his conclusions suspect.

Jake apparently wasn't the only person in the

room with doubts. "Our understanding is that Cutler had special training in wilderness survival, especially winter survival, from his time in the military," Gage said. "He would be more equipped to deal with harsh conditions in the backcountry than most people."

"And we believe he used that training to get him over the mountains and into Utah, where we hope to apprehend him shortly."

The deputies exchanged looks. Clearly, there was nothing else they could do. "Thank you for your time," Sherrell said. "Now you can get on with your regular duties."

"That's all for now," Travis said, and after a few seconds' hesitation, they shoved back their chairs and filed out of the room.

"I hope he's right and Cutler is in Utah," Deputy Jamie Douglas said.

"Or maybe he just wants everyone to think that's where he is," Deputy Ronin Doyle said.

"If he is still up there, he won't sit around and do nothing," Gage said. "He'll break into a cabin or vandalize some property and we'll hear about it."

"Or he'll kill someone else," Dwight said. "I'd just as soon not find out he's still here by responding to another murder."

Jake clenched his jaw so tightly it ached. He

was thinking that he hoped the person Cutler went after wasn't Hannah, but he couldn't say it.

"We'll all be keeping our eyes and ears open," Gage said. "We can't devote manpower and resources to an all-out search anymore, but that doesn't mean we stop looking." He turned to Jake, as if reading his thoughts. "Don't go up in the high country alone. If a couple or three of us decide to go cross-country skiing or drive up to check out some mine ruins on our own time, there's nothing to prevent us from doing so. Solo outings up there are a bad idea anytime, but especially with the possibility of an armed fugitive who hates cops on the loose. Understand?"

Jake nodded. "Yes, sir." He'd be careful, but he wasn't going to let down his guard on the FBI's say-so. There was too much at stake.

AFTER HELPING CLEAN up at the rescue site, Hannah drove to SAR headquarters for the usual review of the rescue and to help put away gear. "Want to come with us to Mo's?" Sheri asked when the meeting broke up.

"Thanks, but I have something else to do," Hannah said.

"Something with a certain good-looking deputy?" Sheri teased.

"Maybe."

"I thought you two had been spending a lot of

time together." Sheri nudged her with her elbow. "Good for you. He seems like a good guy."

"Yeah. I think so."

She had been tired when she left SAR headquarters, but the thought of seeing Jake again energized her. Back at the inn, she headed to her room to shower and change. Her dad stopped her on the stairs. "Everything go okay on your call?" he asked.

"It went great, Dad."

"I heard it was a climber."

"Brock Franklin. Do you know him?"

Thad shook his head. "There are so many new people these days. Is he going to be all right?"

"He's going to be fine." She thought so, at least.

"What happened?"

"I'm not sure. His line came loose. He said he made a mistake."

"It happens to the best of us," Thad said. "I'm glad he's okay."

"Me too, Dad."

"And you're okay?"

"I am." She patted his arm. Today had been stressful, but she'd gotten through it and that had felt so good.

She cleaned up and was downstairs in time to greet Jake when he entered the lobby. Dressed in jeans and a soft blue shirt, he definitely looked good. And smelled good, too. She sniffed his spicy aftershave, but resisted the urge to bury her nose against his neck.

Good thing, since her father spoke from behind her. "Hello, Jake. No Gus?"

"I'm crate-training Gus and he's doing pretty well," Jake said. "I thought it was safe to leave him alone at my place for a few hours."

"I don't suppose you have any news about Charlie Cutler?" Thad asked.

"The FBI thinks he's in Utah," Jake said. "He told his cell mate in Albuquerque that's where he intended to go. We know he has family and friends there."

"Do you think they're right?" Thad asked.

"I don't know," Jake said. "But I figure the feds have information they don't necessarily share with us."

"It would be a relief to know he isn't around here anymore," Thad said, stating the obvious.

"Good night, Dad," Hannah said, as she slipped into her jacket. "Don't wait up."

"Have a good time, sweetheart."

She slid into the front seat of Jake's Jeep and he leaned over and kissed her, a brief but fervent meeting of their lips.

"What happens now, with Cutler?" she asked, as he started the Jeep.

"The FBI is in charge. We won't let down our guard, but there's not much else we can do." He glanced at her. "Try not to think about it too much. Maybe the feds are right. That would be good news."

She nodded. She wanted to believe Charlie Cutler was out of her life, but after so many days of fearing him around every corner, it was hard to turn off that vigilance with the blink of an eye.

"How was your day?" Jake asked.

"Just the usual," she said. "I helped save a guy's life, and rode a stretcher one hundred feet straight out of an icy gorge."

"This, I want to hear all about," he said.

He drove to the Thai restaurant and over pineapple fried rice and spicy prawns she told him about the callout to Caspar Canyon. "Is he going to be all right?" Jake asked when she was done.

"I think so," she said. "We got to him quickly and though his injuries are severe, he should recover completely, unless something showed up at the hospital that we couldn't pick up on."

"Your dad told me he was injured climbing there a few years ago," Jake said. "He said you were on the call. That must have been hard."

"It was," she said. "I was still a trainee and though I'd seen some pretty bad things in training, it's different when it's your dad." She laid down her fork. "I really thought he was going to die and I couldn't handle the idea."

"Was the call today hard for you, remembering your dad?" he asked.

She nodded. "I was really nervous, at first. But once I focused on my patient, it was all about him, not me. Keeping that in mind, and knowing that I could do what I needed to do when it counted, that I didn't have to fall apart, made me feel a lot better. Like I've grown and matured."

"Your dad told me he quit competing because it upset you and your mom so much."

"He wouldn't have given it up if he wasn't ready to," Hannah said. "He seems happy now, sticking to local events. And I feel better knowing he's taking fewer risks."

"Ironic, considering the risks you take every day."

"Maybe, but I'm still young. Dad isn't. And don't tell him I said that."

Jake grinned. "I wouldn't dream of it."

They finished their meal and outside the restaurant, she stopped and looked up at the almost-full moon, such a brilliant, pure white against the black sky. "It's such a perfect night," she said.

Jake brushed his warm fingers across her cool cheek. "It's good to see you looking so happy."

"I am happy," she said. "It's beginning to set in that this whole ordeal with Charlie Cutler might be over." She laced her fingers with his and squeezed.

"What do you want to do now?" he asked.

"Let's go back to your place."

His answer was to pull her to his side in a warm hug. A few minutes later, they stood outside the door to his apartment. "Gus isn't carrying on, so that's good," he said as he unlocked the door.

Inside, the silence continued as he switched on more lights, then helped her out of her coat. Hannah looked toward the large crate beside the sofa. "From here, it looks like Gus is sound asleep."

Jake walked over and unlatched the door of the crate. "Hey, Gus." He leaned down to look inside. "We're home."

The dog lifted his head and blinked sleepily, then his tail began thumping hard. "I need to take him out," Jake said as the dog emerged from the crate. "You can come with us or wait here."

"I'll wait here." She sat on the sofa and patted the wiggling dog while Jake clipped on the leash.

"Lock the door behind me," he said, and kissed her, then came back and kissed her a second time, a deeper, more sensual kiss. "Just to give you something to think about," he said.

She was still tingling with the aftereffects of that kiss once Jake and the dog were gone. Restless, she strolled around the room. It was a simply furnished, clean space, without a lot of personalization. No house plants or photos on the wall. Was that because Jake hadn't had time to add these things, or because he didn't intend to be here long enough to bother?

But even that thought couldn't nudge out the happiness that filled her. Today had been such a good day, from the rescue to the news that Charlie Cutler was out of her life, and the dinner with Jake. She wanted to carry that euphoria into the night.

When she heard Jake's key in the lock she was waiting to wrap her arms around him and pull him close. He responded eagerly, pulling her tight against him and deepening the kiss, leaving no doubt of his desire for her.

"I could get used to that kind of greeting," he said when he finally released her. He unsnapped the leash from the dog's collar. "I need to feed Gus. You could wait for me in the bedroom?" He asked the last as a question, as if verifying her intentions.

"That sounds like a great idea," she said.

Jake's bedroom was like the rest of the apartment, furnished only with the basics of a queen-sized bed, a six-drawer dresser and a nightstand. A navy blue comforter draped the bed and the nightstand held only a single lamp and a phone charger. Hannah sat on the edge of the bed—the mattress was firm, but comfortable. But she didn't really care about the bed or the decor. These observations were only a distraction from what was to come.

She debated undressing and slipping under the covers, but that felt like rushing things. They ought to take their time tonight, and get to know each other bit by bit. Undressing could be awkward, or it could be a fun game. Better to make it the latter—a game she was eager to play with him.

He was grinning when he slipped into the room and shut the door behind him. "Gus never had his supper delivered so fast," he said.

He pulled her close and kissed her again—the man definitely knew how to kiss. He didn't simply mash his lips to hers; he made love to her mouth, alternately tender and insistent, awakening every sensitive nerve ending, which carried the message to the rest of her body that she definitely needed to take this further.

She broke the kiss and pulled back to look at him. "You taste like mint," she said. "Did you brush your teeth?"

"Yeah, well, all that garlic at dinner..."

She laughed. "No fair." She covered her mouth with her fingers, but he tugged her hand away.

"I love the way you taste," he said, and proved it by kissing her again.

By the time the kiss was over, he had backed them to the bed, and they fell onto the mattress, still entwined. She began to unbutton his shirt, letting her fingers brush his bare skin, and the crisp whorls of hair on his chest as she did so, then sliding across his firm abdomen, feeling the muscles contract beneath her fingers.

She slid her hands up once more, and pushed the shirt off his shoulders, and kissed the hollow of his shoulder. He was breathing harder now, his own fingers slipping beneath her fleece top, gliding over her skin.

They helped each other wrestle out of the tangle of their shirts, and he nudged her gently until she lay on her back. He began kissing his way along the top of her bra, his tongue teasing at the flesh beneath, until she was panting. He reached around and unsnapped the clasp, then pushed the garment out of the way and drew one sensitive nipple into his mouth. Sensation rocketed through her and she bit back a moan.

He moved to her other breast, and fumbled with the button of her pants. She caressed his back, delighting in the movement of his muscles beneath her touch. When he eased her pants down her hips, she wiggled out of them, then lowered the zipper on his jeans and slid her hand inside the fly to grasp his erection, the sharp intake of his breath, coupled with the feel of him, hot and hard, sending a stab of need through her.

Within seconds, he was naked and pulling her close again, their legs and arms twined as they sought as much contact as possible, warm flesh to warm flesh, mouth to mouth, hands caressing, stroking, grasping. Hannah broke one kiss with her laughter. "What's so funny?" Jake asked, his hand cupping her bottom.

"Not funny." She shook her head. "Just so… wonderful."

He grinned, and buried his face against her neck, nipping and making her laugh all the more with the joy that surged through her.

Then her smile vanished and he kissed his way down her body, every brush of his mouth making her more aware of her need for him. When his mouth reached her center she closed her eyes and gave herself up to the sensation, the heat and tension building. His fingers stroked the inside of her thighs, then moved up her body once more to caress her breasts as his mouth teased and coaxed. She tried to hold back, to make the moment last, but sensation swamped her, her climax overwhelming and wonderful.

He held her for a moment, and she thought she had never been so completely happy, and so utterly drained. And then his erection nudged at her hip and he leaned over to kiss her once more, and she wanted him all over again.

He pulled a condom from a box in the drawer of the bedside table and she watched as he rolled it on, aroused by the sight of him touching himself. She pulled him to her and guided him inside her in a moment that could have been awkward, but wasn't. After only a few moments they found a rhythm that felt good to them both. She gripped his back, then his waist, and watched as desire transformed his expression into a beautiful fierceness. She felt his climax all the way to her toes, and to the top of her head, touching every part of her. She had enjoyed good sex before, but she had never felt more connected to another person.

They lay together for a long time afterward, silent at first, then talking of little things—how much he was enjoying getting to know the people of Eagle Mountain, stories of her early days with Search and Rescue, when she had plenty of medical training but zero skills at rescue. "I guess it's like anything else," she said. "You feel so in over your head at first, and then everything becomes familiar and the next thing you know, you're the old-timer helping to train the rookies."

"I thought there would be more of that here," he said. "That it would take a while for me to find my feet and be accepted. But I guess since every deputy at the sheriff's department does everything, you're all on a pretty even footing from the start. I like that."

The conversation faded and she was drifting to sleep when the buzz of a phone startled her. She struggled to open her eyes and found Jake already sitting up on the side of the bed. "It's mine," he said, and reached down to fish his phone out of the pocket of his pants.

He answered and listened for a moment, making noncommittal noises, then ended the call, placed the phone on the nightstand and lay back down beside her.

"Is everything okay?" she asked.

"That was Sergeant Walker," he said. "He wanted to let me know the FBI has had a positive sighting of Cutler at his cousin's house in Draper, Utah."

"So Cutler really did leave?" She had already wanted to believe it, but this was the confirmation she hadn't even realized she was waiting for.

"Looks like it." Jake tightened his arm around

her shoulder. "I guess we really can stand down."

She closed her eyes. Stand down. Relax. Her life could get back to normal, or as normal as life ever was when you worked Search and Rescue.

Chapter Thirteen

A large color photo of Hannah being lifted with the litter out of the gorge filled the front page of the next edition of the *Eagle Mountain Examiner*, the caption identifying her by name. Thad insisted on framing the photo to display at the front desk of the inn, and some joker tacked a clipping of the photo on the bulletin board at SAR headquarters, a superhero cape drawn in at Hannah's shoulders with red marker.

A much smaller article at the bottom of the page detailed information about Charlie Cutler's sudden appearance in Utah, where, it was stated, authorities expected to make an arrest soon.

A stretch of fair but cold weather led to an increase in calls for assistance from Search and Rescue, as people rushed to the backcountry to enjoy the snow and sunshine. Not everyone who decided to snowshoe into the mountains or skip the lift lines to ski untracked wilderness had the expertise or equipment to take care of themselves. The team was called to rescue a young couple who had taken a popular ski trail, but become disoriented and lost. They had no map or compass and hadn't familiarized themselves with the area before. When Hannah and three others reached them, they were only feet from the trail that would have taken them safely to the parking lot. It was a happy ending to what might have been a disaster, but it was also frustrating that the couple had not done more to look after themselves.

Another day they had to retrieve a man who admitted he had never backcountry skied before, who had gone too far on a trail that was rated difficult, fallen repeatedly and, since he wasn't dressed properly for the weather, had gotten wet and become hypothermic, as well as exhausted. He, too, survived the ordeal with no consequences thanks to Search and Rescue volunteers.

"I didn't sign on to take care of people who are too stupid to take care of themselves," Austen complained as he and Hannah finished up their reports on the hypothermic skier.

"It can be frustrating," Hannah agreed. "All we can do is try to educate people so they don't make the same mistakes next time. And that man could have died if we hadn't been here to help. He had a real emergency, and that's what we're here for."

He scowled, but said nothing more. Hannah predicted he wouldn't last long-term in Search and Rescue. People cycled in and out of the organization all the time. Some couldn't handle the time commitment, some didn't have the physical fitness necessary, some had life events that prevented them from continuing, and others, like Austen, signed on with expectations that differed too greatly from the reality of everyday wilderness rescue. The work required a passion and dedication that not everyone possessed. Hannah hadn't truly believed she would be a good fit for the work when her coworker had persuaded her to give it a try but to her surprise, she had found a place in the group. She could truly say if she gave it up, she would miss it, even the hard, grueling days, and the days when her best efforts couldn't save an injured person, or the days when by the time SAR was called, it was already too late. And yes, even the days when she ended up rescuing someone who should have had the sense to stay home.

And then there were the calls that took everything out of you—every bit of physical stamina and mental courage and technical skill. Those were the calls that challenged and exhausted you and in the end, made you feel that you had made such a difference that all the suffering had been worthwhile, and you would do it all over again.

"Nobody should kid themselves—this is going to be tough." That was how Tony greeted the volunteers who assembled at the base of Mount Baker shortly after 1:00 p.m. on a Saturday afternoon. Hannah had been getting ready to meet Jake to drive into Junction to take in a movie and dinner, and maybe hit up a club when the call came. Jake hadn't balked or complained when she called to cancel—she supposed one advantage of dating a cop was they accepted that emergencies happen.

"According to the 911 call, we've got a skier stuck on a ledge on the west side of Mount Baker, about two hundred feet below the summit," Tony continued. "He fell skiing down that couloir that runs down the right side of the front face of the mountain."

"He fell there and he's alive?" Ryan asked.

"His partner says so. He was able to communicate with his friend where he lay on the ledge, then he climbed back up to the summit, got a cell signal and called it in. The skier—" Tony consulted his notes. "His name is Jeremy Prather, forty, from Junction. The guy with him is Vick Balin, also from Junction. Vick says Jeremy was conscious, but in a lot of pain, but was able to convey that he thinks he fractured his femur, and may have done some damage to his knee and some ribs."

"I think I know that spot," Ryan said. "I've climbed that route in the summer. It's going to take us at least four hours to hike up there—probably more, depending on conditions."

"What about a chopper to take a couple of medical people up there to triage?" Danny asked.

Tony shook his head. "We don't know what kind of condition the snow is in up there. Even if we could get a chopper over before dark, if the snow is unstable, a helicopter could bring it all down right on top of the guy."

"So we hike in," Ryan said.

"Right," Tony said. "And we don't rush. No sense any of us getting hurt, too. We know setting out this is going to be a night operation, so we take our time and do it right. Ryan, you lead, since you know the trail. Hannah, you and Danny decide what medical equipment we need to haul up there." He called out the names of other personnel and assigned each of them to specific duties.

Hannah and Danny convened in front of the medical supplies. Danny was already pulling items from the bins. "We'll need splints. An air splint. Supplemental oxygen." He began checking off items as he piled them on the table in front of them.

"He'll need pain meds," Hannah said.

"Right. Do we have any medical history on this guy?"

"I don't think so," Hannah said. "But he was healthy enough to be up there skiing."

She retrieved the key for the locked cabinet where they stored their supply of drugs, and reviewed what was available. Taking too much or the wrong things was a waste, but keeping the patient as comfortable as possible was a priority. Tony hadn't mentioned a head injury, which would make treatment easier, but until someone was able to examine the man, they would have no idea of the true extent of his injuries.

Thirty minutes later, Hannah was seated next to Tony in the front seat of the Beast, barreling down a snowpacked county road toward the trailhead at the base of Mount Baker. Ryan and Eldon were fifteen minutes ahead of them, intending to set out to pack the trail and clear any obstacles. Sheri, Danny, Ted, Austen and Chris rode in the rear of the Beast, crowded in with an intimidating array of equipment, from an aluminum litter and oxygen canisters, to a large orange vacuum mattress that reminded Hannah of a swim float. Every bit of that equipment would have to be transported up the mountain on the backs of the rescue volunteers.

Tony parked at the trailhead with the headlights of the Beast illuminating the start of the trail, which from this vantage point appeared to be a narrow, muddy track heading straight up through thick forest. Hannah and the others climbed out and began unloading their gear. No one said much as they worked. This was when Hannah saw the real value in the hours of training. They had been through similar situations before and knew what they had to do. She stifled a groan as she eased into her pack, which must have weighed forty pounds—more than she was used to carrying.

She reminded herself that the others were carrying at least this much and more. Sheri even had the vacuum mattress strapped to the back of her pack, adding two feet to her height. They started up, and before they had traveled a hundred yards Hannah was sweating in her heavy parka, various muscles and joints complaining from the strain. *Think about the patient,* she told herself. *Think about Jeremy.* How was he handling the pain? Was he warm enough? Was he in shock? Was he terrified, lying there injured on the side of a mountain in the dark? She would be afraid in that situation, though she would have one advantage over most other people. She

would know that down here at the bottom of
the mountain a whole team was working to get
to her, to do everything they could—including
risking their own safety—to make sure that she
was all right.

JAKE WAS DISAPPOINTED his date with Hannah had
been canceled, but he wasn't surprised. It might
as easily have been him calling her to say he
had to report in to work to handle an emergency.
They would get together again soon. In fact,
they had scarcely been apart since the night she
had stayed over at his apartment. They weren't
actually living together, but close. The inten-
sity of their relationship surprised him, but it
felt right. More right than anything he had experienced with any other woman.

The big drawback to all those good feelings
was that right now he was worried. She hadn't
given him many details about the call she was
on, though she had mentioned something about
someone having fallen while skiing down a
mountain. "It's going to take a while to get to
him," she said. "So don't expect to hear from
me before morning."

Too restless to sit at home, he leashed Gus
and took him to the park. The dog was more
than happy to accompany him, and spent the
next half hour sniffing every inch of the path

around the perimeter, with special attention to the area around the picnic tables, where he snagged what Jake thought was a chicken wing, though he'd only had a glance at the item before it disappeared down Gus's gullet.

Reluctant to return home just yet, Jake turned toward the sheriff's department. He would just check in with whoever was on duty to see what was going on. Maybe they'd even know something about Hannah's fallen skier.

Deputy Dwight Prentice was the only person in the squad room when Jake and Gus entered. He looked up from his computer at their approach. "Hey. Aren't you supposed to be at the movies or something?"

"Hannah had a callout," Jake said. "Some guy fell off a mountain." He walked to his desk and flipped through the papers in the in-box. "Anything interesting come in?"

"Nothing." Dwight yawned and stretched his arms over his head. "It's a quiet weekend for once."

"Any news from the feds on Charlie Cutler?" Jake asked. "Did they make an arrest?"

"No word," Dwight said. "But then, I'm not sure they'd bother to tell us if they did."

Jake sat at his desk and logged into the computer, then pulled up the files on Charlie Cutler.

"What was the name of that special agent who came and talked to us?"

"Special Agent Sherrell," Dwight said.

"Yeah, here it is." Jake picked up the phone.

"What are you doing?" Dwight said.

"I'm going to call Agent Sherrell and ask him for an update."

"On a Saturday afternoon?"

"Why not?" Jake dialed the number and listened to it ring. Once...twice...by the fourth ring he was expecting a voice mailbox to answer, but instead Sherrell's clear, clipped voice said, "Hello. Who is this?"

"This is Deputy Jake Gwynn in Eagle Mountain," Jake said. "What can you tell me about Charlie Cutler? Did you make an arrest?"

Silence. Jake knew Sherrell was still on the line because he could hear him breathing. "Agent Sherrell?" he prompted.

"No, we did not arrest Charlie Cutler," Sherrell said. "The man we thought was Cutler was actually a cousin who looks very much like him. We brought him in for questioning, but he swears he hasn't heard from Cutler."

Jake felt cold all over. "Are you saying Cutler was never in Utah?" he asked.

"We don't know. We still feel that's where he was headed. All we can say for sure is that Charlie Cutler was not at that house in Draper."

"You don't know where he is," Jake said. "In fact, he's very likely still here in Colorado."

"We don't know that, either," Sherrell said. "Have you had any more sightings of him?"

"We haven't been looking for him," Jake said, his anger barely contained. "You told us not to bother."

"I'm not going to debate this with you, Deputy," Sherrell said, an edge to his voice.

"No, I'm not going to waste time doing that, either." Jake ended the call and sagged back in the chair.

"They didn't get Cutler?" Dwight asked.

Jake shook his head. "The man they thought was Charlie Cutler was a cousin. Cutler probably isn't even in Utah. I bet he's still up there in the mountains. Where Hannah just went on a rescue call." He clenched both hands into fists, wishing he could punch Sherrell—though that wouldn't do anyone any good, he knew. Except it might feel good, to let off some of his frustration. The feds had been so sure they knew better than a bunch of small-town cops.

"Hannah isn't up there alone," Dwight said. "She's surrounded by a whole team of people. People who care about her. Cutler isn't going to get to her, even if he did find out where she was. And I don't see how he would."

Jake nodded. "You're right. She's not alone

and she'll be fine." He stood and snapped his fingers. Gus, who had been napping beneath the desk, jumped up, tail wagging.

"Where are you going?" Dwight asked.

"I think I'll drive out to the trailhead at the base of Mount Baker," he said. "See how things are going, and if they need any help."

To Dwight's credit, he did not remind Jake that Search and Rescue did not need the help of someone who had been on exactly one training exercise, or that Jake would be unlikely to even see, much less speak to, Hannah, who would be busy doing her job. But he could at least pass on the information that Charlie Cutler might still be at large in the area and they should all be on guard.

And on the slim chance that Cutler might show up, Jake wanted to be there, armed and waiting for him.

Chapter Fourteen

If the climb up the mountain had been challenging in the fading daylight, as darkness descended it became the stuff of nightmares. Hannah switched on her headlamp, but no matter how she tilted the beam, it could illuminate only a small area in front of her, spotlighting the orange mass of the vacuum mattress on Sheri's back, or the gleam of the metal oxygen canister carried by Danny, or the steep drop to one side of the trail, or a tree root that tripped her as she passed, sending her forward hard on her knees, or the bare branch of a tree just before it slapped her in the face.

A third of the way up the trail they encountered snow, mixed with mud at first, then slick with ice, and finally thick and fluffy, though Ryan and Eldon had done their best to pack it down. Walking was treacherous, especially when she was unable to see her feet. One inch off the narrow packed path and she would sink to her knees, the heavy pack throwing her off balance and wrenching her sideways. Soon her ankles and knees and hips and back ached and she wanted to scream in frustration. At this rate they wouldn't reach the top of the mountain until daylight.

"Here, grab this. It will be easier." Sheri turned and guided Hannah's hand to a stout rope at the side of the trail. "Ryan and Eldon fixed this up for us," she said.

The rope made the going much easier, and she appreciated having something to hold on to, an extra insurance against plummeting off the side of the mountain. Every hundred feet or so they would stop and wait while Ryan or Eldon pulled the rope up and reattached it, but the pauses allowed them all to catch their breath, and they made better time overall.

The trail flattened for a bit and Tony called for them to regroup. He had left Ted at the trailhead to coordinate from there. "Everybody take a minute to rest, hydrate, get something to eat," he said. "How's everyone doing?"

They all muttered variations of "okay" and "all right." No one wanted to be the first to complain. They were all tired and sore, but also aware that a man lay injured at the top of the mountain, whose life depended on them gutting it out and soldiering on. Hannah leaned against a rock outcropping, letting the rock take some of the weight of the pack. "You can take that pack off if you want," Danny said, coming to stand beside her. "I'll help you get it back on."

"No," she said. She was afraid if she removed the pack, she wouldn't have the strength to face putting it on again.

"Look at the moon," he said, and pointed toward a mountain peak across from them, and the silver edge of the moon just beginning to appear from around the side of the peak. "Another hour or so and it will be all the way up. It will make walking easier."

She realized it was already lighter, their figures casting shadows on the snow. She hugged her arms across her chest, cold. Now that they had stopped, the sweat she had worked up on the climb was chilling her.

"Unzip the vents on your jacket," Danny said. "You should have done it before we started out."

"Yes, Dad," she teased.

"Don't start that," he said. "Just because you don't want me as your lover, you don't have to pretend I'm that much older than you."

"We're much better off as friends and fellow team members," she said. "You know it, even if you won't admit it."

He let out an exaggerated sigh. "You're really hurting my ego here. But yeah. And I'm sorry about what I said at Mo's that night. I was out of line. I was just in a weird place, I guess. Lonely."

The sincerity of his words touched her. "You're forgiven," she said. "And I hope you find the right woman for you. I really do." Danny was a good guy—he hadn't been right for her, but she appreciated that he was her friend.

"Let's head out," Tony called.

"How long have we been hiking?" Hannah asked Danny as they prepared to set out once more.

He pressed a button to illuminate the face of his watch. "About three hours. It's going faster than I thought. It helps that a lot of this trail is in the sun during the day."

For a while the trail wasn't as steep, and they followed a series of cairns across what must have been a scree field in summer, the loose rock and gravel frozen and for now at least, stable beneath a blanket of snow that Ryan and Eldon had packed down for them. The moon bathed them in a soft, white light, adding to the otherworldly feel of the expedition. If not for the struggle to carry the heavy pack, the uncertainty about what awaited them at the top of the mountain and the need to place each step carefully on the uncertain terrain, it would have been a glorious hike. As she trudged along, forcing herself to put one foot in front of the other, to keep going in spite of pain and fatigue and worry, she promised herself she would return in the summer to hike the trail to the top.

She and Jake could come here together. He would be great to hike with—he wasn't a complainer, and he wasn't the type who turned every activity into a competition. He didn't mind taking time to admire the sunset or contemplate the stars. Thinking about him made her smile. She was glad of the darkness, which prevented the others from seeing that smile, which she was sure was the look of a woman who was completely gone for a man she had only known a little more than a month. She and Jake had scarcely been apart since she had spent the night at his apartment. She had been sure at least one of her parents would caution her about not rushing into a new relationship so soon after her split with Danny, but when she had slipped into the inn before breakfast after her first night at Jake's, her mother had only smiled and said, "You look like you had a good time last night," which had both embarrassed and pleased Hannah. Her father's only acknowledgment that something might be going on between his daughter and the new deputy was to remark that he certainly liked Jake and hoped he decided to stay in town.

Hannah hoped so, too. The only shadow in the picture of happiness she was painting with Jake was the knowledge that he didn't see Eagle Mountain as his long-term residence. He had made it clear he intended to move on and move up. Which wasn't to say she couldn't follow him, but everything she loved was here—not only her parents, but her job and her work with Search and Rescue. She could always find another job, but replacing the two sets of people who were truly her family wasn't so easily done.

She gave herself a mental shake. No need to rush things. Her motto from the beginning of this relationship was to take each day as it came. She would enjoy being with Jake but she wouldn't put pressure on him or on herself to make this long-term. Only now that she was a couple of weeks into being with him did she realize how foolish that philosophy could be. It hadn't worked with Danny, and she feared it wasn't going to work with Jake.

But for now, she was stuck—too besotted with him to break up and too fearful that he would leave her to completely lose herself in loving him.

Love. A powerful four-letter word. Neither of them had used it with each other and she didn't intend to. But when she was being completely honest with herself—here, on the side of a mountain in the dark—she could admit she was falling in love with Jake. That felt about as thrilling as walking a ridge of rock with a steep drop-off on each side, and every bit as dangerous.

"ALL I CAN tell you is they haven't made it to the top yet." Ted, the SAR volunteer, was huddled in the front seat of the rescue vehicle, the engine running and the heater on. When Jake had arrived at the trailhead, Ted had invited him to sit with him. "I wouldn't mind the company," he'd said. "This is the most boring part, waiting for the action to begin."

"What happens when they get to the top?" Jake asked.

"If he can get a cell signal, Tony will call me." Ted picked up the phone he had propped in one of the cup holders between the seats. "He should be able to get a signal. The climber's partner called from there."

"How are they going to get up there in the dark, with all the snow?" Jake asked. He couldn't see the mountain from here, but he had a memory of a sharply jutting peak frosted in white.

"They'll figure out a way," Ted said. "A lot of

this work is figuring out things as you go along. I mean, we practice and train for everything we think we might encounter, but there's always something new. It's what makes it exciting and keeps it interesting. And of course, people are always figuring out new ways to hurt themselves, so that keeps us on our toes."

"You haven't seen anyone else around, have you?" Jake asked.

"You mean like lookie-loos? That happens in summer sometimes, but when it's dark and cold the onlookers tend to stay away."

"You really get people who show up at the scene of a rescue to watch?" Jake asked.

"It can be pretty exciting when we're, say, pulling someone up out of a canyon or doing a whitewater rescue on the river."

"How do they know to show up?" he asked.

"They listen to the emergency channel. Anybody can do it. Used to be you had to have a special scanner or radio. Some people still keep those, especially in remote areas of the high country, but most places you can listen in with an app on your phone."

Jake nodded. He knew people listened to police channels but he hadn't thought about them following search and rescue calls. Was that how Charlie Cutler had known where Hannah would be, those times he had left those items at her car? "You haven't seen anyone else, have you?" he asked. "Anyone on the trail?"

"It's not really the time of year for hiking," Ted said.

"How did the man who was hurt get up there?" Jake asked.

"He and his buddy climbed up the back side of the mountain, hiking over on the saddle that connects Mount Baker and Peak 14. It's pretty narrow and there's a lot of scree in summer and ice in winter, but with proper precautions and good skills, it's doable. Then you can ski down the west couloir all the way down to a big snow-field that comes almost to the state highway. If you park a vehicle at both ends it makes for a long day trip."

"But Search and Rescue didn't go in that way?"

Ted shook his head. "Too risky in the dark, carrying all that equipment. Tony thought about sending a couple of people over there, to try to get to the injured man ahead of everyone else, but he was afraid they'd get caught in the dark. And we don't know why this man fell. Maybe there's rotten snow up there or something. This trail is slower, but safer."

Ted offered Jake a piece of gum and he accepted. "If you're worried about Hannah, don't be," Ted said. "She knows what she's doing and our motto is to always take care of ourselves first. We're not going to be able to help anyone if we're injured ourselves. We'll push ourselves and do things a person without proper training should never attempt, but Tony won't hesitate to call off a mission if he thinks it's too risky."

He didn't ask how Ted knew he might be focused on Hannah. They hadn't been hiding their relationship and there were no secrets in a tight-knit group like Search and Rescue. "That's good to hear," he said.

"Is that the only reason you came out here?" Ted asked. "To check on Hannah?"

He hesitated. He wanted to warn Hannah and the others, but he didn't want to spread information that wasn't true. "There's a possibility Charlie Cutler didn't go to Utah after all," he said. "I wanted to warn Search and Rescue to be on the lookout for him."

Ted nodded. "I'll let Tony know when he calls."

"You don't sound surprised to learn that Cutler might still be here," Jake said.

"I saw both the men he killed. Professional work. He was evading capture, but he wasn't running scared. And he seemed at home in conditions other people would find hostile. I thought he might stick around here at least until snowmelt."

"You talk like someone with law enforcement background," Jake said.

"Special Forces," Ted said. "Afghanistan. Let's just say I've dealt with men like Cutler before."

His tone of voice sent a shiver down Jake's spine. He'd been all wrong about Ted when he thought he was just an easygoing old-timer. Right now, with Charlie Cutler out there somewhere, Jake was glad to have Ted on his side.

"Okay if I wait here with you until you hear from Tony?" Jake asked.

"Suits me. Like I said, I'm glad of the company."

They didn't say much after that, and when the phone rang, it startled them. But it wasn't Ted's phone; it was Jake's. "Hello?" he answered.

"Jake, it's Dwight. Thought you'd want to know about a call that just came in. Folks out on county Road 11 got home late from an out-of-town trip and their cabin had been broken into. The burglar took food and a pistol and a bunch of ice climbing equipment."

"Okay." He waited for Dwight to tell him why he should be interested in this.

"Are you at the Mount Baker trailhead right now?" Dwight asked.

"I am."

"Then you're only a couple of miles from these people's cabin."

"You think this burglar might be Cutler." A chill settled over him.

"I don't know. Ice climbing gear is easy to sell and can bring a lot of money, so maybe it was just a garden-variety break-in. But if it is Cutler, maybe he doesn't want to sell the equipment. Maybe he wants to use it. Tell the SAR crew to keep a lookout."

"I will." He ended the call, and held the phone in his hand.

"I heard most of that," Ted said. "You think Cutler is headed up there after Hannah and the others?"

"I think it's something we have to consider."

"What are you going to do?"

"I have to go into town. There's someone I need to talk to." He opened the passenger door. "Tell Tony what you know. He can decide how to handle things from his end. One thing we know about Cutler is he avoids groups of people. As long as everyone stays in groups, they should be safe. And whatever you do, don't leave Hannah alone."

"We won't," Ted promised.

Jake sprinted to his Jeep, then headed back to town. He hoped he was making the right decision, leaving like this. But he needed help if everyone was going to come out of this safely.

HANNAH COULD NOT GAUGE time or distance in the dark, so she was startled when the line of hikers came to a halt and word was passed back that they had gone as far as they could go. They began unloading gear and Tony summoned her and Danny forward, where an anxious-looking man greeted them. "This is Vick," Tony said. "He was skiing with Jeremy when Jeremy fell."

"One second he was fine and the next he was falling," Vick said. "I thought he was gone, but when I looked over the edge I saw he'd landed on a ledge. Down there." He pointed off in the darkness. "I've been lying here for hours, calling down to him, trying to keep him talking." His voice broke, exhaustion and fear in every syllable.

Danny patted his shoulder. "It's okay," he said. "You did everything you could to help your friend."

"Does Jeremy have any health conditions we should know about?" Hannah asked. "Any chronic illnesses? Does he take any medications?"

"Nothing," Vick said. "He's super healthy."

"Was he complaining of anything before he fell?" Danny asked. "Any shortness of breath or unusual pains?" There was always the possibility that some physical ailment had triggered the fall.

"No. We were having a great time," Vic said. "He was skiing ahead of me, doing great. I don't know what happened—all of a sudden he just went over and kept going." His face contorted, reflecting the horror of the memory.

"You've done a great job staying with him, keeping his spirits up," Danny said. "We've got him now, and we're going to take good care of him."

What might have looked like chaos to someone who just happened upon the scene erupted on the mountaintop as everyone set to work, the many parts of an intricate dance coming together. A team set up flood lights to illuminate the shelf where Jeremy Prather lay on his side, half-curled into a fetal position. He wore black ski pants and parka and a black helmet. One of his skis and his ski poles lay a few inches from his right leg, while the other wasn't visible.

A trio of rescuers began rigging lines to secure Jeremy, the various rescuers who would be assisting him and the equipment needed. Hannah harnessed in and climbed down to the ledge where Jeremy lay. She was glad of the darkness now, because it prevented her from seeing how close to the edge she was standing, and how far the drop would be if she fell. Danny followed, but the ledge itself was so narrow they scarcely had room to examine the injured man. At one point, Hannah stood with her feet on the edge of the rock shelf, the rest of her leaning out into thin air, trusting in the safety harness and ropes to support her.

"Jeremy, my name is Hannah. I'm a paramedic and this is Danny. He's a nurse. We're going to make you a lot more comfortable, very soon."

Jeremy, a heavy growth of black beard standing out sharply from his pale, pale face, stared up at her with sunken eyes and tried to smile. "That sounds good," he rasped.

Carefully, aware there was no way to do this without causing Jeremy more pain, Hannah and Danny examined their patient. "Closed displaced fracture of the left femoral shaft," Danny diagnosed. "At least three broken ribs, but no lung puncture. His left knee is swollen, but hard to tell if there's tendon damage."

Hannah recorded Jeremy's blood pressure, pulse, and oxygen saturation, and they fitted him with a mask and portable oxygen. She drew up a syringe of morphine and administered it, then watched as some of the tension gradually eased from his face. "We're going to need to move you into a litter," she said. "It's not going to feel very good while we're moving you, but once you're secured in there, you're going to feel so much better."

The next thirty minutes were spent fitting the vacuum mattress into the litter, securing the litter to lines, then lowering it to the shelf, where Danny and Hannah carefully maneuvered Jeremy into his new bed. She adjusted the mattress to fit around him, immobilizing the fractures and providing a much more comfortable resting place than the frozen rock on which he had spent the past seven hours. Then they tucked in chemical heat packs and covered him with blankets. "How's that?" she asked when they were finished.

Jeremy smiled up out of his cocoon. "Good. A little too warm, even."

Hannah looked across at Danny, who was hugging himself, shivering. "Should have brought some of those hot packs for us," Danny said.

Her radio crackled. "How's it going down there?" Ted asked.

"Good," she answered. "Jeremy is doing great and we're all secure."

"Great. I've had a conversation with HAATS, along with avalanche forecasters, plus Ryan and I hiked up and had a look ourselves. We think we can bring a helicopter in at first light to lift

Jeremy off the mountain. There's not as much snow up here as I thought, and what there is is stable. It will be safer for everyone than trying to bring him down in the dark."

"That's great." HAATS was the Army National Guard's High Altitude Aviation Training Site. Those soldiers were the best in the world in maneuvering in this terrain and SAR had worked with them before. Hannah hadn't relished the idea of carrying Jeremy—who was a big man—down that steep trail, not to mention the suffering he would have had to endure from the constant jostling on the way down.

"I'm leaving Sheri and Ryan up here to monitor all the lines and ferry down any supplies you might need," Tony continued. "I want you to stay on the ledge with Jeremy, monitor his condition and administer pain meds to keep him comfortable. Are you up for that?"

"Of course."

"I could stay," Danny said.

"You could," Tony said. "But you're six-four and Hannah is five-six. She'll be a lot more comfortable on that ledge than you are."

"I'd manage," Danny said.

"You can stay up top with Sheri and Ryan," Tony said. "Relieve Hannah if she needs it, and help with transport tomorrow. Depending on the weather, that could be tricky."

They had all trained last summer with HAATS on airlifting patients, but the idea of having to repeat the exercise in a real-life situation made her stomach hurt. It took real muscle to wrangle the lines from the helicopter's hoist, and a few extra inches of height wouldn't hurt, either. "Good idea," Danny said. "I'm on it."

Things gradually calmed down after that, as the rest of the crew headed back down the mountain and the four who remained behind—Hannah with Jeremy on the ledge and Danny, Ryan and Sheri two hundred feet above, settled in for a long, cold night. Hannah gave Jeremy a couple of energy gels and some water, and one of the team up top sent a flask of hot soup down to her on a line. That soup was one of the best things she had ever tasted and went a long way toward easing the chill. She settled herself on the few inches of ledge next to the litter, and wrapped a space blanket around her shoulders. The low murmur of conversation from above provided a soothing backdrop, and she was close to falling asleep.

She roused herself to check on Jeremy. His pulse was steady and he slept heavily, exhausted and aided by the morphine. By this time tomorrow, this would all be a memory—an exciting story to tell in the future, when he had cheated death on a mountaintop.

She looked up at the full moon. At this elevation it seemed close enough to touch, and she could make out the shadows of valleys and craters on its surface. She wouldn't forget this night, either, one in which she had pushed herself to her limits, overcome fear and doubt to help save a life. The hardest part was over now. In the morning they'd load Jeremy into the helicopter, then head back down the trail, tired and sore but victorious. She'd go back to the inn, take a long shower, eat scrambled eggs and bacon and toast, and sleep for twelve hours. Then she'd see Jake, and tell him all about her big adventure and make love until she fell asleep again. A good end to a good couple of days. Only a few more hours and she would be there, safe and warm and comfortable and stronger than she had been before.

Chapter Fifteen

"Jake! Is everything all right?" Jake had pictured himself walking calmly into the inn and explaining what he wanted to Hannah's father, but something in his expression must have alarmed Thad. The older man hurried from behind the front counter. "Is it Hannah? Has something happened?"

"Hannah is fine," Jake said. "Search and Rescue is headed to the top of Mount Baker to rescue a climber who fell."

Thad searched Jake's face. "There's something else, isn't there?"

"It may be nothing, but I don't want to take a chance it's something."

"What is it?"

"Charlie Cutler may not have gone to Utah at all," Jake said. "The man the FBI thought was him turned out to be a cousin."

"You think he's still here," Thad said.

"There was a break-in on County Road 11

this afternoon. Someone stole some food and a bunch of ice climbing gear."

"The trailhead for Mount Baker is on County Road 11," Thad said. "What do you think Cutler is up to?"

"The skier who was hurt—he and his friend got to the top of Mount Baker by crossing the saddle from Peak 14 and hiking up a short ways. They were skiing down when he fell. I think Cutler may have a scanner he uses to listen in on emergency calls so he knows where Search and Rescue is headed. He may be planning to intercept them up there."

"Because he wants Hannah." Thad's voice remained steady, though he was very pale.

"I may be wrong," Jake said. "I hope I'm wrong. But I need to go up there and see." He took a deep breath. "And I need ice climbing gear to do it."

"You can't go up there alone," Thad said. "That'll only get you killed. Especially since you don't know what you're doing."

Jake had expected him to say as much. And he was right. "Someone has to do something," he said. "It will take hours to get up the trail Search and Rescue took. We can't get air support up there until morning. I'm afraid if we wait it will be too late."

"I'll go with you," Thad said. "I've traversed

that saddle before. It's not that difficult if you know what you're doing."

"I can't let you do that," Jake said, alarmed. Hannah would never forgive him—and he'd never forgive himself—if he took Hannah's father up on a mountain and got him killed.

"I'm older, but I'm not washed-up yet," Thad said. "I can do this to help my daughter. But we're going to do this right."

Jake nodded. Some of Thad's enthusiasm was infecting him. "I'll do whatever you say."

"Then first thing, we call the sheriff and talk to him. We don't do this without him signing off on it."

"That was my next step, after I talked to you."

Thad put a hand on Jake's shoulder. "You call Travis. I'll go get my gear."

He left and Jake moved to an alcove off the lobby of the inn and dialed the sheriff's direct number. "Hello, Jake," Travis said. "Dwight told me the latest developments regarding Cutler. Do you have something new?"

Jake summed up his theory about Cutler's next move, and his plan to try to intercept him on the saddle between Peak 14 and Mount Baker. "Thad Rogers is coming with me. He's climbed in that area before and I don't have the skill to do it by myself."

"It's too dangerous," Travis said.

"Yes, sir. It is. But I think it's more danger-ous if Cutler attacks the SAR team up there on that mountaintop with no sort of law enforce-ment support."

"Let me talk to Thad."

Jake found Thad in a storage closet just off the front desk. "The sheriff wants to talk to you," he said, and handed over the phone.

Several minutes of intense conversation fol-lowed. Thad's half of the conversation consisted mostly of "Yes, sir" and "I'm sure" repeated over and over. Finally, he handed the phone back to Jake.

"Now that you've put the bug in his ear, Thad's determined to go up there without you," Travis said. "Short of arresting him and lock-ing him in a cell, which I can't really do, I can't stop him. So you have to go with him to look after him."

"Yes, sir." Something Thad had said must have changed the sheriff's mind about letting Jake attempt to intercept Cutler. Maybe because he, like Jake, saw that it was their best chance.

"There's something else you should know," Travis said. "We had a report come in a few minutes ago from another house on County Road 11. One of their snowmobiles is missing off a trailer parked beside their garage. They heard the engine fire up at seven o'clock, but by the time the owners got outside, all they could see was the tail light disappearing into the woods. Dwight drove out there, but didn't see any sign of the machine."

"Cutler could have taken it to get to the trail across the saddle," Jake said. "I understand there's a road leading up there."

"Maybe," Travis said. "The machine that was stolen is a 2019 Polaris Switchback, black."

"I'll be watching for it."

"I'm sending three officers up the trail SAR used to rendezvous with you at the top," Travis said. "If you do spot Cutler up there, avoid him if at all possible. Your job is to protect civilians, not to initiate a confrontation."

"Yes, sir."

"Good luck. And do everything Thad tells you. He has all those climbing medals for a reason."

Jake pocketed his phone. "We're going to do this, then," Thad said.

Jake nodded. "We are."

Thad handed him a pair of heavy coveralls. "Wear something warm and easy to move in under these, but you'll need these for the ride up there."

"My Jeep has a heater, Thad."

"You can't get up that road in a Jeep—not this time of year. We'll go by snowmobile."

Cutler had known that, even if Jake hadn't. Jake was more sure than ever that he was right and Cutler was headed toward the SAR team. "Do you have a snowmobile?"

Thad grinned. "I do. You get dressed while I let Brit know what's up, then we'll get going."

Despite knowing that Thad was an award-winning mountain climber, Jake had not pegged the older man as someone with a daredevil personality. Only when he was riding behind Thad as they raced up the forest service road toward the summit of Peak 14 did he realize he was riding with a wild man. Thad opened the throttle wide and they hurtled up a steep trail marked only by tall orange plastic poles at intervals on either side of the road, a rooster tail of snow flying up behind them. The light on the front of the snowmobile illuminated only a tunnel of landscape, making their path seem impossibly narrow, trees crowding in on either side. But he had to trust Thad to know what he was doing, so he gritted his teeth and held on so tightly his muscles ached.

By the time Thad swung the snowmobile around in a wide, level area near the top of the peak, Jake was shaking with both cold and nerves. He braced himself with one hand on the machine as he climbed off, and waited for his legs to steady. Thad showed no such hesitation. He moved to the back of the snowmobile and began unstrapping equipment. "Leave the coveralls here," he said. "Get into this harness. Here's your pack. Don't forget your ice ax. Do you remember everything I told you?"

"I think so." Thad had given him a quick and dirty crash course in climbing procedures, and had ended the lecture with, "Don't worry too much. I'll do the heavy lifting. You just follow orders and hang on."

"You'll be amazed what you remember when you get in a bind," Thad said.

Jake felt steadier now. He looked at the gear piled at his feet, then around the parking area. "I want to look around a little," he said. "See if anyone else has been up here ahead of us."

Two snowmobiles sat under a tarp at the far edge of the parking area. He guessed these belonged to the injured skier and his friend. But a circuit of the entire parking area revealed another set of tracks in the rougher snow at the far edge of the clearing. An attempt had been made to brush snow over them, but the tracks cut deep in the hard-packed snow. At first, he thought they might be old tracks, made days ago, but when he followed them beneath the trees, he found a black Polaris snowmobile half-hidden behind a large boulder.

Jake took out his pistol and double-checked

that the magazine was fully loaded and there was a bullet in the chamber. He hoped he didn't have to use the weapon, but he would do whatever it took to protect Hannah and the other members of her team. He returned to the snowmobile where Thad was waiting, already harnessed and pack in place. "I think Cutler is up here," he said. "I found a snowmobile hidden over in those rocks." He gestured into the darkness. "From what I can tell in the dark, it matches the description of the one that was stolen."

"He won't be expecting anyone to have followed him in the dark," Thad said. "If we're lucky, he'll be so focused on his destination that he won't look behind him and see our lights."

"If he does, and he's still got that rifle with him, we'll be easy enough to pick off," Jake said. The thought made him queasy, but he pushed it aside.

"Hard to climb with a rifle," Thad said. "Hard to aim steady up there, too."

Jake didn't add that Cutler had trained for missions like this, and that he had a marksmanship medal. Better that at least one of them not realize how much the odds were stacked against him. "Let's go," he said.

Thad checked his phone. "There's a signal up here," he said. "Anybody you want to call?"

Jake hesitated, then said. "Yeah. Yeah, there is."

HANNAH WAS STARTLED when her phone rang. Vick had told them he had to climb up the mountain to get a signal strong enough to call for help. The team had been communicating via radio, and she hadn't thought to check her phone. Everyone she knew should be asleep at this time of night. She was going to be really annoyed if some spammer was interrupting her on the top of a mountain in the middle of the night. But when Jake's name flashed on the screen, she smiled. Leave it to him to be thinking about her. "Hey," she answered. "What are you doing up this late?"

"How are things going up there?" he asked. "Everything okay?"

"Calm as can be," she said. "My patient is stable and cozy and I'm enjoying the view, safely roped in on a ridge a couple hundred yards from the summit."

"Who is with you?"

"Danny, Sheri and Ryan. The National Guard is sending over a helicopter at first light to airlift our patient. Then we'll have to hike down."

"I don't want to frighten you," Jake said. "But we think Charlie Cutler may be headed your way."

Her breath caught at the name she hadn't expected to hear. "He's supposed to be in Utah," she said. "He's supposed to be in custody by now."

"The man the FBI thought was Cutler turned out to be his cousin. Someone stole a snowmobile and some climbing gear this evening. We think it was Cutler, and he's headed your way."

"How would he know where to find me?" The idea was incredible—and horrifying.

"I think he probably listened in on a scanner," he said. "One of the cabins he broke into probably had one—some of those emergency radios with weather bands have police bands, too."

"I can't believe this is happening."

"I'm going to call Tony and tell him, but I wanted you to hear it from me first. I'm on my way across the saddle between Peak 14 and Mount Baker. I don't think I'm that far behind Cutler."

"Jake, you can't make that climb by yourself! Especially not in the dark."

"It's actually really bright up here, with the full moon, and I'm not by myself. I have a very experienced guide with me."

Something in his voice made the hairs on the back of her neck stand up. "Who?"

"Your dad. He's the most experienced climber I know and he insisted on coming with me."

"Nooooo," she moaned.

"I have to go now. Let the others know what's

going on. If you know Cutler is coming, he won't be able to sneak up on you. And he's always avoided groups before, so you have that in your favor."

"Jake?"

"I'm still here."

"Promise me you'll be careful. I… I don't want anything to happen to you."

"I'll be careful. You, too. Remember I love you."

The call ended before she could reply. Her heart pounded, his words echoing over and over. *Remember I love you.*

"I love you, too," she said, then keyed the mic button of her radio. SAR trained for all kinds of situations so that they'd be prepared in the case of a real emergency. But having a serial murderer headed toward you through the darkness wasn't the kind of thing anyone could prepare for.

THE MOON ON the snow was so bright Thad declared they didn't need their headlamps. "That will make us a little less obvious if Cutler does look over his shoulder," he said, as he double-checked Jake's harness. "Though if we were doing this like the 10th Mountain Division in World War II, we'd dress all in white. Then we'd be invisible against the snow."

"Let's hope Cutler didn't think of that," Jake said. Though the murderer had supposedly gone through the same training that had been developed for the original Tenth Mountain Division troops in World War II, he didn't think Cutler had access to winter camouflage.

"White's not a popular color for outdoor gear," Thad said. "People want to be visible, so it's unlikely he found any to steal." He tugged on their lines. "I'll lead the way. We won't hurry. Follow in my footsteps. If you fall, self-arrest with your ice ax like I showed you."

Jake's stomach heaved at the thought of falling, but he merely nodded, and followed Thad out onto the icy ridge between the two mountain peaks. The first few yards were much like walking any icy trail, and Jake gained confidence as his crampons bit into the rough surface of the ice. But as they progressed farther, the trail narrowed to less than a foot wide, the ice whipped into rough peaks by the wind, so that every step was at an angle. He stared down at his feet and gripped the ice ax in his right hand, suddenly fearful of dropping it and seeing it spin out into the void on either side of the trail.

"Breathe." Thad's voice drifted to him, soft and clear. "This looks a lot scarier than it is."

Jake nodded and tried to do as instructed,

though his breath caught in his throat, his lungs refusing to completely fill.

"I think you were right and someone is ahead of us," Thad said, again speaking softly. "There are fresh tracks."

"Can you see him?"

"No. The terrain is pretty uneven. Don't worry about him right now. Worry about getting across this middle section. It's the trickiest."

Jake decided that no one who wasn't desperate or had a death wish would voluntarily cross that icy ridge. The rough, crusty surface crumbled at every step, and he felt his ankle wrench as he flailed to keep his balance. "Easy," Thad called back to him.

When Jake felt steady again, he looked ahead to find the older man regarding him calmly. "You're doing great," Thad said. "Come to one of my clinics at the ice festival and I'll show you some really exciting stuff."

"This is excitement enough for me," Jake said. Movement beyond Thad's shoulder caught his attention. "Down!" he hissed, and crouched low. The small, dark figure was at least a hundred yards ahead, moving swiftly across the ridge. So far, he didn't appear to have noticed his two pursuers.

"I don't think he's seen us," Thad whispered. Jake shook his head. He squinted, trying to bring Cutler's figure into sharper focus. He didn't see the outline of a rifle. Did that mean Cutler had, indeed, left that weapon behind? He wouldn't go unarmed, but he had stolen a handgun from one of the houses on County Road 11, so maybe he had that with him. "We need to get closer." Close enough to be within shooting range of Cutler. Jake would give the man a chance to surrender, but he wouldn't let him get within striking distance of Hannah and her friends. Cutler had proved he was ruthless—Jake would be just as ruthless.

Chapter Sixteen

"What are we supposed to do—just sit here waiting for this maniac to take us out?" Even over the radio Hannah could hear the tremor in Sheri's voice.

"Is there somewhere up there you can take cover?" Hannah asked. "Behind some rocks? Anywhere you're less visible?"

"We're already in a kind of niche between some boulders," Ryan said. "We settled in here to be out of the wind."

"Then stay there," Hannah said.

"What about you?" Danny asked.

"He's not going to see me down here," Hannah said.

"All he has to do is follow all the ropes," Danny said. "You should come up here with us."

"I'm not going to leave Jeremy." The idea of leaving this seriously wounded man to whatever Cutler decided to do, while she ran and hid, appalled her.

"He's stable and sleeping, right?" Danny said. "He won't even know you're gone."

"I'll know I left him," she said. "And I won't do it. Besides, his pain meds are going to wear off in the next hour or so and I'll need to give him more."

"I'll come down and stay with him then," Danny said. "Cutler doesn't give a rip about me. You're the one he's fixated on."

"No." She couldn't shake the idea that giving up her post here would put the others in more danger. She didn't want Cutler to find them first and take his anger and frustration out on them.

"What have we got that we can use as a weapon?" she heard Sheri ask in the background.

"Rocks," Ryan said. "Rope. Hey, I have a grappling hook. That would make a good weapon."

"Not against a gun," Danny said.

"If we see him first and take him out we'll be fine," Ryan said, with more bravado than Hannah could have managed.

"We need to stop talking, in case he hears us," she said. "You know how sound carries up here."

"What is Jake doing about this?" Danny asked.

"He and my father are hiking over across the saddle," she said.

"Are they out of their minds?"

"Dad thinks they can do it safely."

"Maybe twenty years ago. Thad isn't a kid anymore."

"Don't tell him that. He'll say he can still out-climb you any day of the week."

"He'd be right," Danny said. "But I'm not much of a climber. And Jake isn't a climber at all, so what's he doing risking his life that way?"

"You'll have to ask him when he gets to you." Jake and her dad would reach the others, she told herself. She wasn't going to entertain any other possibility. She signed off and checked her watch. Three fifteen. Another three hours before the beginning of sunrise. How long after that before the helicopter could be here?

And how long until Charlie Cutler arrived?

"Is something wrong?"

The question, from Jeremy, surprised her. "Hey." She knelt beside him. "How are you feeling?"

"Hurting again." He licked dry lips and she found the water bladder she'd placed under the blankets to keep it from freezing and directed the bite valve to his mouth.

"I can give you another shot in about forty-five minutes," she said. "Can you hang on until then?"

"Yeah." He frowned. "I heard you on the radio. What's wrong?"

How much to tell him? There was nothing he could do to help. "We're just coordinating personnel movement," she said. "Your ride to the hospital should be here in another four hours or so."

"You people are amazing," he said. "I've never seen anything like it."

"You're pretty amazing yourself," she said. "A lot of people wouldn't have survived the fall you took."

"Where's Vick?"

"We sent him down with the rest of the crew. He didn't want to leave you, but he was exhausted."

"He's the best. He kept me from panicking, and then talked to me while we waited for you guys to arrive. I don't know what I would have done if he hadn't been there." He laughed, which turned into a cough. "I'd probably be still lying here, freezing to death," he said.

Maybe. Or he might have hung on until morning, when someone missed him and called for help. In her short time with Search and Rescue, she had seen some miracles. She had also seen people who didn't make it. That was the part she hadn't considered when she signed on with the group—that there were days and weeks where the job was more body retrieval than life saving. She always reminded herself during those times that those bodies were important to their families, so what they were doing was also important, if not nearly as satisfying.

"You must be tired yourself," Jeremy said.

Physically, she could feel exhaustion pulling at her, a heavy weight around her shoulders and ankles. But she was far too keyed up to let sleep overtake her. Especially after that phone call from Jake. "Tell me about skiing down mountains like this," she said. "Have you done it before?"

"I've skied this mountain before," he said. "Two years ago. Everything went perfect that time."

"Have you been hurt before?"

"Never. I guess I was overdue for my luck to run out."

"Do you think you'll do it again?"

"Ask me again in a few months. Or ask my wife. I guess I wouldn't blame her if she insisted I stick to lift-served terrain from now on." His voice grew thick. "She's pregnant, with our second child. Maybe it's past time I started playing it a little safer."

They talked about his little boy, his job as

a systems analyst, his wife and how they met. He was in a mood to talk, and Hannah didn't mind listening, though one ear was always attuned for other sounds—the scrape of a boot on rock, the rattle of debris raining down from above. The stealthy approach of someone who shouldn't be up here.

At four o'clock she administered another injection of morphine and Jeremy drifted off. She checked the vacuum mattress and adjusted his blankets, then settled back, one hand wrapped around the syringe in her pocket, the empty hypodermic needle the only weapon at her disposal. If Cutler was set on slitting her throat, as he had his other victims, she was determined to fight back.

JAKE SPENT LESS time focused on his feet now, and more time watching for glimpses of Cutler ahead of them. "He's moving really fast," he said.

"Faster than I'm comfortable going," Thad said. "We're going to catch up with him soon enough."

What would they find when they did?

They had progressed only a few feet farther before Thad pitched forward. The sudden hard tug of the rope that linked them made Jake stagger, and brace against the strain. He stared as Thad grappled at the slope with his ice ax. "What can I do to help?" Jake called.

"Just…stand there. Don't move."

A few moments later, Thad staggered to his feet beside Jake. "Are you okay?" Jake gripped the older man by the shoulders.

Thad nodded, breathing hard. "It's good to know I still know how to do that," he said after a moment.

"What happened?" Jake asked.

"I think our friend up there knows we're following him after all."

"Why do you say that?"

Thad switched on his headlamp and turned to train the light down on an abrupt dip in the trail. "I think he hacked out a section of the trail," he said. "I didn't notice in time and slipped. Probably took a year or two off my life, but I'll be okay."

"Can we get around it?" Jake asked.

"Just step carefully. We'll be fine. But be on the lookout for other booby traps."

They found the second trap fifty yards farther on—a slick sheet of ice four feet across, glinting in the moonlight. "He must have dumped all the water he had down here," Thad said.

They traversed this section on hands and knees, crampons and ice axes providing traction. "How much farther to the summit of the mountain?" Jake asked when they were upright again.

"That's it up there." Thad pointed ahead, to an uplift of bare rock that reminded Jake of a broken shark's tooth.

"How long will it take us to get there?" Jake asked.

"Half an hour. Maybe forty-five minutes?"

"How far ahead of us is Cutler?"

Thad looked ahead at the dark figure that slipped in and out of view. "I'd say he's almost there," he said. "Then he'll have to climb down to the SAR team. Didn't you say they're a couple hundred yards below the summit?"

"Yes."

Thad nodded. "The down climb will take more time. We'll get closer to him then, maybe catch him in midclimb, when he's more vulnerable."

It was hard to think of Cutler as being vulnerable. Since his escape he had assumed mythic proportions. *He's just a man*, Jake reminded himself. *He's made mistakes before, and been caught. He can be caught again.*

Jake only hoped no one else died before Cutler was back in custody.

Someone was moving around above. The crunch of crampons on ice was faint but clear in the still air. Careful not to tangle her safety line, Hannah levered herself up on hands and knees and climbed over the litter and pressed herself into a narrow space between the litter and the mountain, the chill of the bare rock seeping through the layers of her clothing like an icy finger tracing her spine. She waited, holding her breath, ears straining. The silence was so complete she might have believed she had suddenly lost her hearing.

Suddenly, a scream rent the air, and sounds of struggle. Heart in her throat, Hannah strained her ears to make out what was happening. Her radio crackled and she groped for the transmit button in the dark. "What's happening?" she whispered.

"He's here," Sheri gasped. "He got Ryan. Oh God, Hannah, I'm sorry."

The radio went dead. "Sheri! Sheri!" Hannah tried again and again to raise her friend, but the only reply was ominous silence.

Chapter Seventeen

"Help! Oh God, please help!" At first Jake thought the woman who slammed into him was Hannah, but when he was able to pull back enough to look at her, he realized it was her fellow SAR member, Sheri.

"It's okay," he said. "You're okay."

"Sheri, what's happened?" Thad asked.

She looked from one man to the next, her eyes growing a little less glazed. "Charlie Cutler's here," she said. "We'd been watching for him. Listening for him. We were hiding and didn't think he could sneak up on us, but he did." Her words became more rushed, her voice higher pitched. "He came out of nowhere, and he had a knife. He slashed at Ryan and Danny and just…just *shoved* them off the mountain. They were clipped into safety lines, which should have saved them, but Cutler looked right at me, then he…he…" She shook her head, the words choked off by sobs.

Thad pulled her close and held her. "It's all right," he said. "You don't have to tell us."

But she did. Jake needed to know everything Cutler had done since his arrival on the mountaintop. "What did he do?" he asked, keeping his voice gentle.

"He cut the safety lines," she said. "He just bent down and cut the lines, then kicked the ropes over the side. He was watching me the whole time he did so and I'll never, ever forget the evil in his eyes." She buried her face against Thad again.

"Did he hurt you?" Jake asked.

She shook her head. "He took a step toward me and I ran. I didn't look where I was going or anything. I just unclipped my own safety line and ran. I remembered Hannah had said you and her dad were headed this way, so I ran this direction."

"Cutler let you go," Jake said. If the killer had wanted Sheri dead, Jake was sure Cutler would have followed her. "He wants us to know for sure that he's here."

"I tried to warn Hannah," Sheri said. "I radioed her but then I dropped the radio. She's down there on that ledge with Jeremy, who's too injured to do anything to protect her. Oh God, Cutler will probably kill him, too." She began sobbing again.

Jake patted her shoulder. "Stay with her, Thad," he said.

"What are you going to do?" Thad asked.

"I'm going to try to stop him." He drew his pistol. "Where is Hannah, exactly?" he asked Sheri.

She raised herself and sniffed, pulling herself together. "You'll see the ropes we rigged, and a pile of gear and stuff. She's over the edge on a ledge maybe a hundred feet down."

"There's nothing to stop Cutler from picking her off with a gun," Thad said, his voice strained.

"He's never shot any of his victims," Jake said. "He's used a knife on all his other victims." He would try that with Hannah, too, but to do that he had to get close to her. He'd have to climb down that ledge. But he wouldn't make it to her if Jake had anything to say about it.

"Don't think you can hide from me. I know you're down there." Hannah had never heard Cutler's voice before, but she knew it was him. He didn't sound anything like she expected. Instead of the deep, menacing growl she had given him in her imaginings, he had a higher pitched, pinched sort of voice.

"I've been looking forward to meeting you," he said when she didn't answer. "I can't wait."

He chuckled and she closed her eyes, willing herself not to be sick. She gripped the syringe more tightly in her hand, wishing she had thought to fill it with a very large dose of morphine. Enough to knock him out. That was completely against regulations, but surely she could be forgiven.

She stifled a gasp of hysterical laughter. How absurd to be thinking about licensing regulations at a time like this.

"I hear you," Cutler said. "Are you laughing or crying? It doesn't matter. I'm coming down. But first, I need to get rid of a few obstacles." A few seconds later a length of rope slid down, pooling on the litter where Jeremy lay, snoring lightly. A second coil of rope followed. "There," Cutler called. "You won't need those safety lines anymore."

A shower of rock followed, then a boot appeared, and Cutler was climbing down another length of rope with the ease of someone moving down a stepladder. She shrank further into the shadows, aware she was trapped, hemmed in on one side by a wall of rock and on the other by the litter, and beyond that the fall into a deep gorge, from which her body might never be recovered.

Cutler smiled at her, an expression that sent a shiver through her, his eyes so lacking in warmth, so distant even as he stared right at her. She turned her head, not wanting to see those eyes anymore. "Just give me a minute," he said. "Let me make a little more room." He bent down and shoved at the litter.

"No!" she shouted, realizing he intended to push Jeremy off the ledge.

Cutler straightened and turned to her once more. "She speaks." Again, the awful smile.

"Don't hurt him," she said. "I… I'll cooperate with you, but don't hurt him."

"You will cooperate," he said. "You won't have any choice. But if you like, I'll leave your patient for later." He beckoned. "Come here."

"How did you get here?" she asked. "How did you know I'd be here?" She didn't care about the answer; she only wanted to keep him talking. Jake was on the way. All she had to do was keep Cutler talking, keep him focused on her, until help arrived.

"I listened to the scanner," he said. "Once I knew your location, I made sure I had what I needed to get up here."

"You've been stealing from summer cabins and the ski huts," she said.

"People are very careless with their belongings," he said. "And far too trusting. A couple of those cabins didn't even have locks on the doors."

"You left that bandanna on my car," she said. "And the candy wrapper."

"I wanted you to know I was thinking about you. Were you frightened?"

Did he want her to be frightened? Would saying no enrage him? "I was frightened," she admitted.

"Come here," he said, his voice more forceful now.

She looked down. There was nowhere else to place her feet.

"Step on him. It won't matter to him after a moment."

She wasn't going to step on a man with a broken leg. Instead, she stepped on the edge of the litter, closer to Cutler, but still out of his reach.

"We need more room," Cutler said. He bent and grasped the side of the litter again.

"No!" She screamed the word, which echoed across the canyon below.

"Cutler! Freeze!"

Her heart lurched as she recognized the voice behind the command. Cutler looked up. "Go away, Deputy," he said, the calmness with which he spoke chilling. "Unless you want to see this woman die."

"I have a gun trained on you," Jake said. "Make a move and I'll kill you."

"And risk putting a bullet in an already injured man? Or in Hannah?" He lunged and grabbed her wrist and yanked her forward with such force she might have been a rag doll pulled along by a child. He wrapped a powerful arm around her and held her to his chest.

"Let her go!" Jake sounded more desperate than forceful now.

Something stung Hannah's neck and she closed her eyes, realizing she was feeling the very sharp blade of a knife. A knife like the ones Cutler had used to slash the throats of his other victims. The knife he intended to use on her. She curled her hand around the syringe in her pocket, which she had not let go of since this ordeal began. If she stabbed Cutler with it now would he use the knife on her? And how would she get one small-gauge needle through the layer of winter clothing he wore? She sagged, her knees suddenly jelly.

"Don't faint on me," Cutler said, hauling her upright against him. "It's so much better if you're awake for the whole process."

Process? He thought of murder as a process? The rage this idea engendered banished her weakness.

"Are you still there, Deputy?" Cutler called.

No answer. Cutler hugged Hannah more tightly. "I guess he left," he said. "I can't see him anymore. Looks like it's just you and me."

She shivered as his lips brushed the side of her cheek.

"Cutler!" Jake's shout echoed across the canyon. Cutler jerked his head up as a heavy grappling hook hurtled toward him. He tried to dodge the missile, and brought the hand that held the knife up to shield his face. He still held Hannah, but his grip loosened enough for her to half turn in his arm, and bring the needle up, burying it in his eye.

With a cry of rage he released her. The grappling hook caught him in the shoulder, snagged in the fabric of his parka and held. Hannah grabbed hold of the rope Cutler had climbed down on and began to haul herself up, even as Cutler tried to drag her back.

A shot rang out and Cutler roared again, but released her. Then Jake was pulling her up, into his arms. He held her tightly with his free hand, the other still holding the pistol. "Are you all right?" he asked.

"Yes." She nodded. "But we have to get Cutler away from Jeremy. He was trying to push the litter off the ledge."

Thad and Sheri ran up to join them. Jake indicated the rope the grappling hook was attached to. "Hold on to that and don't let go," he said. He holstered the pistol and picked up the rope Hannah had climbed up.

"What are you going to do?" she asked.

"I'm going to arrest Cutler."

"Jake, no!" But he was already climbing down.

JAKE KNEW THAT Cutler was pinned by a grappling hook in the shoulder, with a gunshot wound in the other shoulder. And he had a hypodermic needle in one eye. The combination ought to have disabled him enough for Jake to get handcuffs on him, but he knew better than to count on it. If he had been able to choose, he would have waited for help to arrive before confronting the murderer, but Hannah's insistence that Cutler wanted to push the litter with Jeremy Prather aboard into the canyon forced him to take action.

His boots touched the ledge, but he held on to the rope until he was standing steady and had his bearings. The light of his headlamp illuminated Cutler, crouched against the rock less than five feet away, clutching his shoulder, blood staining his parka. He had managed to remove the hypodermic from his eye, and free himself from the grappling hook, which hung between them, the sharp, curved tines of the hook hanging at eye level, menacing.

Jake stared at the hook, fear climbing his throat. He forced his gaze away and met Cutler's eyes, shining in the beam of his head lamp. "You're no match for me, Deputy," Cutler said, the nasal whine of his voice like fingernails on a chalkboard.

Jake didn't answer, but raised the gun. "Don't move or I'll shoot."

Cutler sprang to his feet and lunged for the hook as Jake fired, but the shot went wild, the bullet flying out into the emptiness over Cutler's right shoulder. Cutler clawed at the hook and Jake dropped the gun and grabbed hold of one curved prong with both hands as it swung toward him. He staggered as Cutler pulled back on the hook, and had the terrifying sensation of one foot struggling to find purchase in thin air.

"One shove and goodbye, Deputy," Cutler said.

Jake kicked out, hard, and caught Cutler square in the chest, sending him staggering back. While Cutler struggled to regain his balance, Jake crouched and retrieved the gun. He trained it on Cutler, one hand holding the weapon steady, the other clutching the grappling hook. "Don't move," he said. "You're under arrest."

Cutler's eyes were wild with fury. Jake was sure the other man would rush him again, and tightened his grip on both the pistol and the hook. But Cutler turned, not toward Jake, but away, and just as Jake pulled the trigger Cutler leaped off the ledge. He disappeared without a sound, but the thud of his body hitting the rocks below was unmistakable, and sickening.

Jake's legs gave way and he sat, his back against the rock, and stared at the man in the litter in front of him. Jeremy Prather opened his eyes. "Who are you?" he asked.

"Nobody important," Jake said, and closed his eyes. He was suddenly very tired, and determined to wait here and not move until someone else arrived to take charge.

"Jake!"

Hannah's voice roused him. "Jake, are you all right?"

He struggled to his feet, realized he was still holding his pistol, and shoved it back into the holster. "I'm fine," he said. "And Mr. Prather is fine."

"What happened to Cutler?" This question was from Thad.

Jake swallowed. "He jumped." The sound of Cutler's body hitting the rocks would haunt him for the rest of his life.

"I should come down and check on Jeremy," Hannah said.

"Come down, then."

"We need to set new safety lines," Sheri said.

"Jake, you need to help Hannah with the ropes. She'll show you what to do."

Later, he would try to come to terms with what had just happened, but for now it helped having something to focus on that required his full attention. They fixed the new safety lines, Hannah checked her patient, who was fine, then Jake and Hannah embraced. They didn't say anything for a very long time, just held each other. He breathed in the scent of her hair and tried to memorize this sensation of her in his arms.

They could have stood that way for hours, but screaming from above startled them apart. "Sheri!" Hannah called. "Sheri, what's wrong?"

"It's Danny! He's alive!"

Jake and Hannah scrambled up to the others, to find Danny, obviously battered but standing upright, with one arm around Sheri. "He just came climbing up the backside of the ridge," Sheri said, tears streaking her face.

"What happened?" Hannah asked.

The others filled her in on Cutler's earlier attack, relating how he had shoved Danny and Ryan off the mountain and cut the safety lines. "I landed hard in a big snowfield," Danny said. "Had to swim my way out, then got pretty beat up on the rocks climbing back up. I was still attached to the other end of the rope he cut, so

I managed to tie a rock around it and throw it around a jagged outcropping and use that to help me climb up. I tried yelling but I guess everyone was so focused on Cutler they didn't hear me."

"Don't you ever say you're not a very good climber," Hannah said. "You're an amazing climber."

"But what happened to Ryan?" Sheri asked.

The question cast a pall over their celebration. "I don't know," Danny said. "I called for him and looked around the snowfield where I landed, but he wasn't there."

"We'll have to look for him as soon as it's light," Hannah said.

"When the helicopter flies in for Jeremy, we'll ask them to look," Danny said, his expression grim. "Maybe they'll be able to spot him from the air." He didn't say "spot his body" though Jake thought that was what they were all thinking.

"What time is it?" Hannah asked.

But before anyone could answer, a phone rang. Sheri pulled out her cell phone. "Hello, Tony," she said. "You're missing all the excitement."

She listened a few moments. "Okay," she said. "We'll be ready." She ended the call and tucked the phone away. "The helicopter is on the way," she said. "ETA thirty minutes."

"You didn't tell Tony about Ryan," Hannah said.

"It didn't seem like the kind of thing to mention on the phone."

"Come on." Danny put a hand on each of the women's shoulders. "We've got work to do."

"Anything I can do to help?" Jake asked.

"No offense," Danny said. "But stay out of the way. I'm not being rude. When that Blackhawk lowers that cable it's the most dangerous part of the whole operation. That thing can take a man's head off."

They heard the helicopter long before they saw it. It came at them from the west, a speck the size of a fly hovering in the distance and gradually growing larger, the sound of its rotor rising to a roar so that they had to shout to be heard. Jake did as instructed and remained well out of the way on the summit, watching as Hannah, Sheri and Danny maneuvered the cable and attached a tag line, dodging the menacing hook and fastening the litter with a finesse he was sure looked much easier than it actually was.

The helicopter lifted up and away from the mountain, and the litter rose up into the belly of the aircraft, then the chopper swung away, headed east. "While I was in radio contact, I asked them to look for Ryan," Hannah said.

No one said anything for a long ten minutes as they contemplated the potential loss of their fellow volunteer, or perhaps the ordeal that had just passed. Then Sheri's phone rang again. "Hello?"

She jumped up, her face transformed. "They spotted Ryan!" she shouted. "And he's alive. Hurt, but alive." She listened again. "Yes, sir, but…yes, sir." She hung up the phone. "There's a fresh squad coming up to handle Ryan's rescue. Jeremy is stable, so the Blackhawk is going to hang around to help."

"What do we do now?" Jake asked.

"We collect our gear and head back down," Hannah said. She looked to Danny. "Are you okay to make it down? I noticed you're favoring your ankle."

"I'll be fine," he said, and began coiling rope.

Twenty minutes later they had almost everything packed up when Sheriff Travis Walker, Deputy Jamie Douglas and Deputy Shane Ellis reached the summit. Travis looked them over. "Everybody okay?" he asked.

"Yes, sir," Jake said. "Everyone but Cutler."

"What happened to him?"

"He jumped. I guess he was serious about never going back to jail."

Travis shook his head, but said nothing else. Jake would provide a full report later. Sheri explained they were expecting another rescue squad to arrive shortly to set about taking care of Ryan, and the sheriff and his deputies agreed to stay until the new rescuers arrived, in case they could be of assistance.

Then Sheri, Thad, Hannah, Danny and Jake started down, moving slowly, carefully. No one spoke for a long time, then Sheri tilted her head to the sun. "I feel like I should go to church and light a candle," she said. "I've never seen so many miracles in one day."

"We should have a new motto," Danny said. "Eagle Mountain Search and Rescue—Miracles at No Extra Charge."

Hannah looked over her shoulder and smiled at Jake, and suddenly, he didn't feel as tired and sore. Maybe finding her hadn't been a miracle, but it had been an unexpected blessing, one he would never take for granted.

Epilogue

Ryan hadn't fared as well as Danny in his plummet from the mountain, having broken his ankle and his shoulder in the fall. But the second rescue squad got to him quickly and was able to effect a second lift with the Blackhawk, which carried its double load of the wounded to a trauma center in Salt Lake.

Search and Rescue conducted a third mission near Mount Baker three days later, to retrieve the body of Charlie Cutler, which had been located in a ravine on the mountain's west side. Austen and Ted rappelled into the ravine and secured the body to the hoist of a helicopter that lifted it out. Hannah was just as glad to be spared that duty. Instead, she received a call from Vick Balin, who told her Jeremy had undergone surgery to put a metal bar in his leg, was healing well and expected to make a full recovery. "You people were angels up there," Vick said. "Absolute angels."

"It was an amazing experience for all of us," she said, and Vick didn't know even half the story. Danny and Ryan surviving being tossed off the summit of Mount Baker would go down as a SAR legend, and already the bad jokes were circulating about not trusting Hannah with a syringe.

Word was that Jake was in line for a commendation for his bravery on the summit, though he modestly dismissed the idea. "The SAR volunteers were the true heroes that day," he said. "And Thad Richards. I never would have made it across that ridge without him."

When told he would receive a commendation, too, Hannah's father was speechless. The reporter had chosen that moment to take his picture, and this newspaper clipping had been added to the wall beside the checkout desk at the Alpiner Inn, along with the image of Hannah riding the stretcher out of the icy gorge. The picture showed Thad standing between Hannah and Jake, an arm around each of them, looking a little stunned.

Even though Jake dismissed the commendation as "no big deal," Hannah insisted they celebrate, so he took her to dinner at a new steakhouse in town, situated in a new building that had been made to look old, which featured lots of antiques on the walls and a bar full of exotic whiskey. "I hope the steaks are as good as they seem to think they are," Jake said after studying the menu.

Hannah laughed. "They have homemade pie, too. You deserve a splurge, don't you?" she asked.

"I know you do, and that's good enough for me." He set aside the menu, avoiding her eyes. He'd been acting a little distant all evening, and it was beginning to ruin her appetite.

"Is something wrong?" she asked. "You've been acting strange all evening."

He picked up his fork and turned it over. "Nothing's wrong, exactly," he said.

She swallowed, and tried to steel herself against whatever was coming. The expression on his face didn't portend anything good. "What is it?"

"I got a call from Colorado State Patrol today," he said. "They offered me a job."

She caught her breath. "That's good news, isn't it? Isn't that what you wanted?" Her voice broke and she blinked rapidly, but not fast enough to hold back the tears.

"Hey." He leaned over and took her hand. "What's wrong?"

She shook her head, then picked up her napkin and dabbed at her eyes, noting the black streaks of mascara on the white linen. "I don't want you to leave."

"Who said anything about leaving? I'm not going anywhere."

She looked up, stunned. "You turned them down? Jake—"

"I told them I'd only take the job if I could stay in Eagle Mountain."

"Why is that?" she asked.

"Because this place feels like home. I have friends here. I have an apartment I like, and I have Gus." He squeezed her hand. "I have you."

"But that was your dream job," she said.

"It's still my dream job." He shook out his napkin and spread it in his lap. "I start next month. The reason they offered me the job was because they want another officer on this side of Dixon Pass. One of the supervisors saw an article about what happened on Mount Baker and thought I was a good candidate for the job, familiar with the locals and the country around here." He grinned. "I didn't bother mentioning I've only lived here three months."

She laughed, as much from relief as amusement. "You've made the most of those three months," she said. "Making all those friends and adopting a dog. Finding that great apartment."

"Finding you," he said. "All of that other stuff I could replace, not you."

"Gus is irreplaceable," she chided. Now that he'd had some training, Gus was shaping up to be a great dog. Jake was even talking about teaching him search and rescue work.

"Okay, maybe that's true. But you're the reason Eagle Mountain is home for me now." He brought her hand to his lips and kissed it. "I love you, Hannah," he said. "Everything that happened on Mount Baker just made me realize how much."

"I love you, too, Jake." She stood and leaned across the table and kissed him.

That was how the server found them, clinging to each other over the table. He cleared his throat and they sheepishly pulled apart. "Something to celebrate?"

"We have a lot to celebrate," Hannah said. A whole future of adventures together, and a chance to fall even more deeply in love.

* * * * *

Don't miss the continuation of Cindi Myers's Eagle Mountain Search and Rescue series next month!

Get 4 FREE REWARDS!

We'll send you 2 FREE Books plus 2 FREE Mystery Gifts.

FREE
Value Over
$20

Both the **Harlequin Intrigue®** and **Harlequin® Romantic Suspense** series feature compelling novels filled with heart-racing action-packed romance that will keep you on the edge of your seat.

YES! Please send me 2 FREE novels from the Harlequin Intrigue or Harlequin Romantic Suspense series and my 2 FREE gifts (gifts are worth about $10 retail). After receiving them, if I don't wish to receive any more books, I can return the shipping statement marked "cancel." If I don't cancel, I will receive 6 brand-new Harlequin Intrigue Larger-Print books every month and be billed just $6.24 each in the U.S. or $6.74 each in Canada, a savings of at least 14% off the cover price or 4 brand-new Harlequin Romantic Suspense books every month and be billed just $5.24 each in the U.S. or $5.99 each in Canada, a savings of at least 13% off the cover price. It's quite a bargain! Shipping and handling is just 50¢ per book in the U.S. and $1.25 per book in Canada.* I understand that accepting the 2 free books and gifts places me under no obligation to buy anything. I can always return a shipment and cancel at any time by calling the number below. The free books and gifts are mine to keep no matter what I decide.

Choose one: ☐ **Harlequin Intrigue Larger-Print** (199/399 HDN GRA2)   ☐ **Harlequin Romantic Suspense** (240/340 HDN GRCE)

Name (please print)

Address   Apt. #

City   State/Province   Zip/Postal Code

Email: Please check this box ☐ if you would like to receive newsletters and promotional emails from Harlequin Enterprises ULC and its affiliates. You can unsubscribe anytime.

Mail to the Harlequin Reader Service:
IN U.S.A.: P.O. Box 1341, Buffalo, NY 14240-8531
IN CANADA: P.O. Box 603, Fort Erie, Ontario L2A 5X3

Want to try 2 free books from another series? Call 1-800-873-8635 or visit www.ReaderService.com.

*Terms and prices subject to change without notice. Prices do not include sales taxes, which will be charged (if applicable) based on your state or country of residence. Canadian residents will be charged applicable taxes. Offer not valid in Quebec. This offer is limited to one order per household. Books received may not be as shown. Not valid for current subscribers to the Harlequin Intrigue or Harlequin Romantic Suspense series. All orders subject to approval. Credit or debit balances in a customer's account(s) may be offset by any other outstanding balance owed by or to the customer. Please allow 4 to 6 weeks for delivery. Offer available while quantities last.

Your Privacy—Your information is being collected by Harlequin Enterprises ULC, operating as Harlequin Reader Service. For a complete summary of the information we collect, how we use this information and to whom it is disclosed, please visit our privacy notice located at corporate.harlequin.com/privacy-notice. From time to time we may also exchange your personal information with reputable third parties. If you wish to opt out of this sharing of your personal information, please visit readerservice.com/consumerchoice or call 1-800-873-8635. **Notice to California Residents**—Under California law, you have specific rights to control and access your data. For more information on these rights and how to exercise them, visit corporate.harlequin.com/california-privacy.

HIHRS22R2

Get 4 FREE REWARDS!

We'll send you 2 FREE Books plus 2 FREE Mystery Gifts.

FREE Value Over **$20**

Both the **Harlequin® Desire** and **Harlequin Presents®** series feature compelling novels filled with passion, sensuality and intriguing scandals.

YES! Please send me 2 FREE novels from the Harlequin Desire or Harlequin Presents series and my 2 FREE gifts (gifts are worth about $10 retail). After receiving them, if I don't wish to receive any more books, I can return the shipping statement marked "cancel." If I don't cancel, I will receive 6 brand-new Harlequin Presents Larger-Print books every month and be billed just $6.05 each in the U.S. or $6.24 each in Canada, a savings of at least 10% off the cover price or 6 Harlequin Desire books every month and be billed just $4.80 each in the U.S. or $5.49 each in Canada, a savings of at least 13% off the cover price. It's quite a bargain! Shipping and handling is just 50¢ per book in the U.S. and $1.25 per book in Canada.* I understand that accepting the 2 free books and gifts places me under no obligation to buy anything. I can always return a shipment and cancel at any time by calling the number below. The free books and gifts are mine to keep no matter what I decide.

Choose one: ☐ **Harlequin Desire**
(225/326 HDN GRTW)

☐ **Harlequin Presents Larger-Print**
(176/376 HDN GQ9Z)

Name (please print)

Address   Apt. #

City   State/Province   Zip/Postal Code

Email: Please check this box ☐ if you would like to receive newsletters and promotional emails from Harlequin Enterprises ULC and its affiliates. You can unsubscribe anytime.

> **Mail to the Harlequin Reader Service:**
> **IN U.S.A.:** P.O. Box 1341, Buffalo, NY 14240-8531
> **IN CANADA:** P.O. Box 603, Fort Erie, Ontario L2A 5X3

Want to try 2 free books from another series? Call 1-800-873-8635 or visit www.ReaderService.com.

*Terms and prices subject to change without notice. Prices do not include sales taxes, which will be charged (if applicable) based on your state or country of residence. Canadian residents will be charged applicable taxes. Offer not valid in Quebec. This offer is limited to one order per household. Books received may not be as shown. Not valid for current subscribers to the Harlequin Presents or Harlequin Desire series. All orders subject to approval. Credit or debit balances in a customer's account(s) may be offset by any other outstanding balance owed by or to the customer. Please allow 4 to 6 weeks for delivery. Offer available while quantities last.

Your Privacy—Your information is being collected by Harlequin Enterprises ULC, operating as Harlequin Reader Service. For a complete summary of the information we collect, how we use this information and to whom it is disclosed, please visit your privacy notice located at corporate.harlequin.com/privacy-notice. From time to time we may also exchange your personal information with reputable third parties. If you wish to opt out of this sharing of your personal information, please visit readerservice.com/consumerchoice or call 1-800-873-8635. **Notice to California Residents**—Under California law, you have specific rights to control and access your data. For more information on these rights and how to exercise them, visit corporate.harlequin.com/california-privacy.

HDHP22R2

Get 4 FREE REWARDS!

We'll send you 2 FREE Books plus <u>2 FREE</u> Mystery Gifts.

FREE
Value Over
$20

Both the **Romance** and **Suspense** collections feature compelling novels written by many of today's bestselling authors.

COUNTRY LEGACY COLLECTION

19 FREE BOOKS IN ALL!

Cowboys, adventure and romance await you in this new collection! Enjoy superb reading all year long with books by bestselling authors like Diana Palmer, Sasha Summers and Marie Ferrarella!